I SWEAR
BY APOLLO

Margaret A Ogola

Focus Publishers Ltd

I Swear by Appollo
First published in 2002 by
Focus Publications Ltd
P O Box 28176
00200 Nairobi, Kenya
email:focus@africaonline.co.ke

ISBN: 9966-882-72-3

Printed by English Press
P O Box 30127
Nairobi

This book is for Vincent Wambugu
who has taught me how to believe again
and for John Felix Odongo—ever and
always loved.

Contents

Contents

ONE

WANDIA

THE FLAME-TREES, their flowers the colour of newly spilt blood, stood sentinel by the main avenue connecting the library and the lecture theatres of the College of Humanities, Design and Fine Arts, a recent additional campus to the University of Nairobi. It had been designed and built by some of the leading architects in the country, who had outdone themselves in trying to make it an institution worthy of its name. The buildings were magnificent without being overwhelming or gaudy—with a fine and well balanced beauty about them, something that could hardly be said about many of the buildings in the thrusting young city of Nairobi, where glass and concrete vied with each other to see which combination got the prize for glaring ugliness.

The spacious grounds of the campus were studded with excellent sculptures including some pieces from the grand master Elimo Njao—made after the terrible fire which had razed down his world-famous gallery, Paa ya Paa, which had contained some of the finest works of art to be found anywhere.

The College was the kind of place any truly artistic soul would feel at home and had been the brain child of the first woman president of Kenya while she was still the minister of education in the previous government.

Her excellency, who had taken over the presidency in a coalition government after the unsung demise of the former incumbent, was a tough and fearless woman known to have faced down armed policemen—at a time when the law of the jungle was rife. She was also a darling of the international community and the intellectual fraternity. Therefore, the college thrived as did many other institutions which had all but sunk into miserable decline and decay after years of mismanagement and deliberate sabotage.

She had made many Kenyans dare to dream again, to hope again. Of course she had many avowed enemies, especially those who had brought the country to its knees through massive institutionalised corruption. She had treated them with the same ruthlessness with which they had raped the country before bleeding it dry. Many were in jail, but some had escaped and were biding their time in exile. Many were surprised that a woman could bring such cold ferocity to the art of governance. She seemed to have an instinct for the jugular and was not afraid to use it.

The corrupt hated her guts and prayed for her demise daily.

On a fine May morning, a girl, with a hand-woven *kiondo* basket slung over one shoulder, walked down this main avenue of the campus with her face being alternatively thrown into shade and light. It was a striking face with a well moulded bone structure, heart-shaped and ending in a rather pointed chin. She had a small but broad-based nose which more than anything else indicated her part-African ancestry. Her mother had been an African woman from around the region of the Great Lake that nestles in the heart of Eastern Africa and her father was English Canadian. Rather than being merely beautiful she was unusual.

Her skin was mellow honey, but the most arresting thing about her, were her eyes. They were a rich brown, flexed with slate-grey spicules radiating around the irises; occasionally they betrayed so haunting a depth that one felt an almost corporeal pain on coming in direct contact with them. It was as if one had been wounded by something as unsubstantial as a ray of innocent light. Her smile, though arresting, was distracted and infrequent. Her personality was withdrawn, almost hidden and she was full of contrasts—perhaps because she had been brought up by a woman of rare excellence who in fact had somehow managed, with the dexterity of a skilful physician [which in fact she was], to heal wounds which would otherwise have been mortal, but which had nonetheless left rather deep scars.

The girl was a twenty-four-year-old post-graduate student of music at the College of Humanities and was in the process of defending a learned dissertation on *The Evolution of Music and Dance Among The Peoples Of Eastern Africa*. Music was the medium in which she lived her life, the impulse which moved her soul. She played several instruments with perfection. As a teacher of music she could inspire almost any group of students to extraordinary performance, injecting pathos and beauty and nostalgia for a lost past into even the most energetic traditional song and dance.

Though she was reserved and withdrawn, men were attracted to her in an irresistible but paralysing sort of way—as if they must destroy themselves in order to achieve actualization, like the final ecstasy of a moth in a flame. They flocked to her or rather to her vicinity, but then remained tongue-tied, racking their brains as to what to do or say next in the face of such passivity— she seemed to generate no currents whatsoever and met every proposition with a slight, amused smile and a look which conveyed nothing more than an empathic recognition of another soul in this vale of tears. To know her would be to know all the joys and sorrows of manhood, and that woman, though so obviously accessible, was not only unknown, but was essentially unknowable.

At the age of eighteen the girl had undergone a minor rebellion. Compared to the seismic upheavals that tend to over-take many adolescents, it was nothing at all. Nonetheless it was irritating that one so liberally endowed with physical perfection, should wear nothing but nondescript skirts and plain blouses. It is after all a natural and universal desire to adorn—even that which is already excellent, perhaps more so. It was as if her very soul shied away from ostentation or even merely attracting attention to herself—as if she must negate some long forgotten aspect of her life. But then again most people do bring to the present a tenuous and very often complex past and she was no exception.

Her brother John, generally known as Johnny, teased her in the rather merciless way brothers have, even though he loved her not merely in a brotherly way—which is rare enough—but with the understanding gentleness born of once shared suffering. Johnny had a rather exuberant personality, but was capable of an uncanny depth at times. The two, brother and sister, had been brought up by their uncle and aunt after their divorced mother had died and their father had failed to reclaim them. Thus the unusually strong bond that bound them together.

Johnny himself had undergone a titanic crisis of identity which he had only resolved by rejecting a part of his being, a course of action much frowned upon by the wise woman who was both aunt and foster mother to him. She insisted that harmony could and must be found in remaining open to all the positive potentialities within one's being. But Johnny had simply felt unequal to the kind of balancing act and long drawn, unresolved pain that his sister seemed to be able to exist with. He was rather like his uncle in this—he preferred clean-cut solutions with no grey areas. Sometimes in those rare moments of self-knowledge he would admit, in his secret heart, that he was taking the easy way out. But he tried not to dwell on such things—there was after all, the exciting world of medicine to explore and as for attention from the girls, a man could hardly ask for more; he was, to put it modestly, a very good looking young man even though he was rather pale for someone who aspired to be totally African and whose mother had after all been African.

"Give yourself a break, Alicia!" He would often tell his sister. His English had a deliberately pronounced Nairobi accent which he had never tried to soften at all - with slurring of the consonants and an exaggerated accent on the last syllables, indeed he was only waiting for a scientific breakthrough on how to make his reluctant melanocytes produce more pigment, at which point he felt his transformation to full African would be complete. Johnny also spoke fluent Swahili, which was no thanks to his aunt who was a lame duck when it came to that mellifluous and demanding tongue. Most impressive of all, he had a reasonable stock of at least one tribal language—the *Luo*—the acquisition of which must have required extraordinary resourcefulness since John had been brought up in an entirely *a-tribal* atmosphere. His uncle Aoro (his mother's brother) was Luo, while his aunt Wandia was Kikuyu; and the language used at home was mainly English with a smattering of street Swahili—a mode of speech having little to do with the real thing.

"What kind of a break?" Alicia would ask with an innocence all the more infuriating because it was real. It made her brother terribly apprehensive on her behalf. Really, how was a person like that supposed to survive in this world where even the sheep wore wolves clothing under their skins and were even more voracious and cunning than the more regular sheep-suited canines?

"What do you mean—what kind of a break! I mean look at you and the way you dress! What do you have against yourself? A girl like you should have the entire Y-chromosome population at your feet!" She would merely gaze at him with that expression of a hurt too bewildered and deep to be comprehended and which caused even he, who should surely be inured by now, real pain.

"But I don't want anyone at my feet."

"You are hopeless," he would say throwing up his hands dramatically, but he would be back at her in a few days. Alicia, regarding the goings on of the human race from the secrecy of her heart, thought that to have any of the men she knew at her feet would be tantamount to having a secret death-wish. They all struck her as ravenous. Delicately, she felt round the edges of her soul and finding them intact, came to the conclusion that though she sometimes felt too afraid to live, she however did not want to die. There must be some meaningful thing or person to which or to whom she could commit herself and thus find self actualisation and peace. She longed for peace.

She was quiescent but not peaceful, yet people confused the former with the latter. For example her aunt Wandia was a very peaceful person, however she was anything but quiescent. She had well defined opinions and was always ready to express them, even the more unpopular ones, if the need ever arose. She had a thoughtful and productive mind, yet was recollected and tended toward a calm solitude. She was helpful and demanding, but had the inner strength needed to let others map out their own destiny without cramping their style with unnecessary interference. Come to think of it there was something almost oriental in aunt Wandia's approach to life, a kind of calm acceptance at least of those things that had to be or needed to be. The positions others took never seemed to make her feel threatened or uncertain.

"In some ways," she had once said to Alicia, precisely in regard to her brother Johnny, "each man is an island and must therefore make his own mistakes. Of course we must hope that we survive our mistakes, but sometimes we don't. What will be will be."

***

PROFESSOR WANDIA SIGU, long-serving chairperson of the Department of Pathology and a forefront authority on diseases of the blood, was known to her neighbours simply as Mama Danny—a title she cherished more than any other and which simply meant 'the mother of Danny'. This afternoon found her sitting at her desk marking essays written by her post-graduate students. The subject matter was 'the treatment of haemolytic blood diseases.' A few were excellent but most were mediocre. She wondered why it was that the excellent seemed to hone and polish their excellence to ever greater heights while the mediocre seemed to sink deeper into the mire. In any case all that was required of her at this stage was to occasionally give a nudge in the right direction. Those who would, responded while the rest seemed to just fade away.

On the other hand being a mother to Danny was a different story altogether. It had sifted and shaken her. It had plumbed the depths of her soul. It had tested time and again the threshold of her capacity to suffer. In short it had made her more completely human than if she had never been Mama Danny. For Danny was special. She had other children of course whom she loved dearly, but Danny was Danny.

The professor was thus lost in reverie when her foster son (and nephew), Johnny, walked into the study in his usual breezy manner. He was almost twenty-three and was at that stage in his medical career, and life in general, when one is confident, without a shade of reasonable or unreasonable doubt for that matter, that all knowledge was attainable and that all happiness was possible to anyone who would strive after them. And there was no doubt that he was a striver, in fact he thrived on every kind of challenge—physical and intellectual and he generally excelled, and therefore was not lacking in a fair amount of arrogance.

Johnny was also an enthusiastic collector of all manner of pet scientific hypotheses, and apparently the more outlandish the better for him. He cherished most those that were connected with evolution of the mind (a kind of psychological neo-Darwinism), and those concerned with the inbuilt self-destructibility of the little green planet upon which he dwelt, after which catastrophe, only those whose minds had evolved to a certain degree of intellectual and moral excellence would survive to rebuild something better upon the ruins of planet Earth with its rotten politics and corrupt morals.

Johnny sometimes felt that man was beyond redemption. He had watched in horror as his own beloved country sank into a vortex of inefficiency, corruption and filth—figuratively and literally; and as all kinds of misfits struggled for power and when they got it, used it solely to line their own pockets with cash and their bellies with layers of fat. Johnny watched in disbelief as his country, a country with possibly the greatest potential in East and Central Africa and perhaps beyond, was run aground by men who were both inane and vicious; men incapable of grasping the bigger picture—of seeing beyond their avarice. This combined with the machinations of the international money markets, a vicious global economy and ruthless multinationals left Johnny feeling that really there was no hope for modern man.

His aunt, however insisted that there had been other equally terrible times in history and that they had passed—thanks to the common instinct for survival and continual yearning for something better that was hidden in the heart of every person. Of Johnny she said;

"He would die happy if he could convince himself and everyone else that the Universe arose from a big bang and that it will go out the same way, like an exploding light-bulb," Wandia had once remarked to her husband Aoro; but he had a practical turn of mind and true to the spirit of the surgeon he was, he did not like anything which could not be palpated, cut out and examined.

"But what does it matter?" he would wonder. Asking such questions was one reason why his nephew never sought his opinion on purely abstract questions. He, a somewhat heavy set and distinguished looking man in his forties, was more at home discussing tissue-damage, appendectomies, fistulae and the like. He was a first-class surgeon and felt that this was more than enough for him. Existential questions did not appeal to him at all. He was glad to be here and hoped that when the time came for him to depart he would do so without too much fuss.

Wandia, on the other hand, had allowed herself to take an interest in a wide variety of issues. Life, existence, demanded to be examined with more than just a superficial glance, more even than mere scientific speculation. The answer, she had decided, was not in the further fission of the atom, or even the greater manipulation of the nucleic acids upon which were coded the future attributes of the organic individual— for these things could exist, at least for limited periods, in the absence of the principle of *life*. In the case of man, there was also the question of the presence of a rational soul which aspired to *know* that which it needed to *love*.

"Hi Auntie!" said Johnny in his airy fashion, which hid a deep and potentially turbulent personality. "Anything new in the world of blood elements today?"

"I am afraid not, Johnny," she answered smiling. "You are back early today." She stated this last without sounding unduly curious. She had tried to raise her children with the understanding that unless they themselves went out of their way to lose it they would be trusted to handle their lives and their studies in a responsible manner. She could not help but be secretly pleased that even her foster children who were by now old enough to realise that their mother had left them extremely well off financially, still conducted themselves according to the principles of hard work and simplicity which she had instilled in them from childhood. And they all still lived at home even though it meant inconveniences like sharing bedrooms and waiting one's turn to use the bath room. Alicia had of course graduated to the self-contained guest-wing at the back of the main house by virtue of the fact that she had a job at the Conservatory, taught Music part-time in two schools and therefore earned a living and could pay rent. She had, in her quiet manner, allowed her tempestuous cousin, Lisa, to share the place with her.

Lisa was seventeen, and academically precocious, but was at that point in her adolescence where she was practically unlivable with, unless of course one was Alicia, who had the patience of Job himself. Lisa, who had skipped two classes in primary school, was already an undergraduate student—taking a degree in Information Technology. She could make a computer all but spin and dance and do cartwheels. But though Lisa may have had brains, she was neither as wise as a serpent nor as gentle as a dove.

The rest of the house was shared out more or less equally—John with Mugo aged almost fifteen, and a kindred spirit; Danny, with his little brother Gandhi, a seven-year-old fellow who fancied himself some sort of a gangster; or trouble-shooter; or bandit—his mother could never quite tell which, except that he seemed to possess the peculiar ability of turning almost anything, from the most innocuous toy, to his school books, into some sort of a weapon, usually a gun. His mother quite frequently felt like returning him to his maker for an exchange.

The next daughter was twelve-year-old Kipusa whose real name was Anwarite after the saintly

Clementine of Zaire, but who had been dubbed Kipusa, which meant pretty girl, from her earliest childhood. She shared a room with a cousin Ciro (the product of a liaison between Wandia's late brother Timothy and some ambiguous female who seemed to have had no antecedents of any kind). She had disappeared into thin air after Timothy succumbed to the Aids epidemic which had laid a path of desolation across the continent of Africa. So terrible had the situation become that the instinct for survival, if nothing else, had forced men and women to review their sexual behaviour and to at least reign in some of the loose ends.

But for millions of men, women and innocent children the change had simply come too late. Ciro, a lucky survivor, was six and had the peculiarity of looking uncannily like Wandia and the two had taken to each other almost instantaneously. In that large and heterogeneous family she quickly lost her shyness, forgot her unhappy past and simply thrived.

In reality it was not just the Sigu household which had increased in size as a result of the decimation of young adults which had been wreaked by the Aids epidemic. Thousands of families in sub-Saharan Africa had had to take in orphans whose future would otherwise have been bleak indeed. But in spite of this, hundreds of thousands of orphans had not been so lucky as to benefit from these vestiges of the extended family system which had once been the norm in Africa. They simply ended up as street children or village urchins.

The youngest member of the family was Mark, aged two-and-a-half, who had a sunny and loveable—almost angelic—personality. His mother firmly believed that he had purposely and unexpectedly been sent by the Almighty to make up for that mobile disaster called Gandhi. Mark was still young enough to occupy the little bright coloured alcove which opened directly into his parents room.

"Elizabeth would have been very proud of me," Wandia mused often. Elizabeth had been her late mother-in-law dead these many years. They had been very great friends, much to the amusement and sometimes annoyance of her husband Aoro, who had felt that this deep friendship and loyalty between a daughter-in-law and a mother-in-law, if not outrightly unnatural, was at least a flight right into the face of revered tradition which tacitly held that these two people who loved him most should be at frequent loggerheads with each other—with him, of course, as the time-honoured referee and respected arbitrator. At times he had even suspected that the two women occasionally conspired against him! It puzzled him a lot, but how could a man complain that his wife and his mother were as thick as thieves? Elizabeth's death did not improve matters much, for whenever there was a particularly tricky problem in the family, Wandia, instead of consulting his superior wisdom as the eldest living male, would fly off to the farm down at Njoro with the most transparent of excuses, or none at all for Wandia was not a person much given to explaining herself. There she would spend long periods sitting by the grave of the late Elizabeth Sigu.

And all this time I thought that the Kikuyu are a particularly level headed people who were too busy with life to be bothered with the dead, yet here she is communing with the dead like the most tradition-bound Luo praying to his ancestors! Aoro would think to himself, amused and incensed at the same time.

***

JOHNNY'S CONTINUED broad smile brought Wandia to the present. He noticed that his aunt had a particularly professorial air of abstraction today.

"Classes ended early and my unit is not on call today so I thought I might come home early and impress upon everyone what a dutiful nephew I am."

"What of the string of girls who hang on your every word, did you give them strychnine or what?"

"Well, if you must know, they are absolutely no competition when it comes to a chance to exchange a word with you, auntie; you are the only woman I know who has both brains and beauty. I tell you those girls are so empty headed that attempting to have an intelligent conversation with them is like talking to a pussy cat and an idiotic one at that," he proceeded to imitate — 'Oooh how sweet you are Johnny!' "It is

22

enough to make a guy throw up," he added emphatically. Wandia sighed and then laughed in exasperation.

"Your uncle must have told you by now that I am immune to flattery—so if you want your allowance early, you spendthrift, just say so." John made such a comically injured face that his aunt laughed again. He, as a matter of fact, needed an urgent replenishment of funds, though he had not quite managed to come up with a story plausible enough to convince his aunt as to the cause of his severe poverty only a few days after having been given his very reasonable allowance from his late mother's estate.

Wandia never made such occasions easy on a guy. His sister Alicia lived strictly within her means and even managed to save considerable sums of money. Johnny had once accidentally seen her bank statement. It had made him whistle. He did not know that thrift was a quality many women in her lineage had shared. Other kinds of incontinence may have existed, but never financial. Their own mother had amassed quite a lot of wealth by a combination of astute thrift and ruthless acquisitiveness. If thrift and acquisitiveness could be considered virtues, then they were the only virtues she had possessed.

"You are a real nut-case, Johnny. Seriously what do you want, is there a new theory in the air? How many more years before the cataclysm? I would like to make a last will and testament to whoever shall survive."

"Honestly auntie, it may sound like a joke but I was reading this book 'The Hab Theory' and it makes the whole thing terrifyingly likely. The author suggests that every several thousand years the build-up of ice in the north and south poles becomes so great that the earth becomes top-heavy and flips over with almost total destruction of life and civilisation. It is an excellent explanation of the sudden demise of many great civilizations such as the great Egyptian empire and the civilization of the Aztecs."

Wandia regarded her foster son quizzically and then shook her head,

"Why is it that you will believe almost any nonsense except the obvious—that man and the universe were brought into being, an act usually called creation, by an intelligent mind, and for a purpose which, though hidden in the muck of human history, is surely unfolding?"

"Oh that! That is pure myth. It has been displaced by archeology and the carbon dating of fossils."

In fact what he meant, but was unable to explain due to the unexplored chaos in his own soul, was that the haphazard enormity of pain in the world, both moral and physical, was too much to allow for any explanation short of chance or the action of a particularly malevolent intelligence. He had no real problem with causality at all—it was just a place to begin his contention, but like many others before him he had a problem with the *Why?* Wandia who had once been a thorough-going agnostic and consequently had great understanding of the doubts that beset the human mind, said;

"Why more a myth than 'The Hab Theory'? In any case I am talking about the question of initial origins, which is crucial, and not of time-spans which is incidental. The fact that the process may have taken billions rather than thousands of years or even six symbolic days, is impressive only to man with his pittance of seventy years. How can one comprehend the manner in which an exquisite Artist, not bound by time, would choose to create a masterpiece such as the universe? Principles don't change, my boy; and the greatest principle of them all is that 'nothing comes from nothing.'"

The young man gazed into her calm intelligent eyes and suddenly unable to bear any more the pains and contradictions of his own existence and the insistence in those eyes, he averted his. He blustered towards the window of her study and looked out. The two remained silent for a while. The professor was one of those people with whom one could maintain a thoughtful silence for a long time without feeling that one needed to excuse oneself, much less make polite conversation.

"You know Johnny," she began in her mellow voice that made one think of warm sunshine, "I rather think that running away has never been a good way to handle a problem." This apparently irrelevant statement did not appear to surprise Johnny at all and he did not ask her 'running away from what?' Instead he turned towards her once again and whispered;

"But why doesn't he come just once to see us? It is killing me. It has probably killed my sister already." So secure was he in her affection that it never occurred to him that his statement could be misconstrued as ingratitude. He and his sister had after all received nothing but the very best of parental care from his aunt and uncle. Their own parents could hardly have done better.

"I don't think so, Johnny. At least she is handling it, but what you are doing is simply shoving the problem under your subconscious. You must deal with the idea that he may, for whatever reason, never come to you; but that this does not make you a lesser person any more than it prevents you from becoming whatever you want to become."

"You know what I think? I think that he has abandoned us because we are half-black!" He spat these last words out of tightly pursed lips. The professor regarded him in her infuriatingly calm manner. There was even a little smile at the corner of her lips.

"You are a man now, Johnny, and it is unworthy of a man first of all to make such rash judgement without bothering to get sufficient facts; for example, he could be dead. Secondly, I think you are having a rather unmanly attack of self-pity." She was a very understanding and gentle person, but she was known to absolutely loath whining and whiners—she dealt with such persons with a curtness bordering on rudeness. She herself possessed the tensile strength of steel and had the peculiarly feminine virtue of durability to an extraordinary degree.

Johnny could have sulked. He could have resorted to dramatics and stormed out; but this woman had raised him and turned him from being a practically autistic child to a normal out-going healthy boy, despite a few problems—and who hadn't a few? So he smiled, and turned back to gaze at the world with youthful bewilderment.

The boy stood by the window for a long time drawing strength and wisdom from the woman almost as one receives a life-giving infusion. Finally he left—quite forgetting what in the first place had brought him to her study—her sanctum and the only luxury she permitted herself, so that she could think, she said, for she was a woman much given to thought. Whatever it was had paled into insignificance for he had been in the presence of the truly wise. He went off to tackle the world once again and for a while, it was clearly noticeable that his customary bravado was absent and his usually clear and handsome brow was knitted in uncharacteristically deep thought.

Wandia turned back to her papers, but was too distracted to concentrate. Soon she too gave up and turned towards the window to meditate as her nephew had done a few minutes earlier. Finally she got up and paced the small room with unusual agitation. After some time she sat down and pulled out a pad from under a pile of books and slid it towards herself.

She hesitated a moment with the tip of the pen

gripped between her teeth—a habit she had when thoughtful and which she had failed to get rid of despite the fact that everyone in the household old enough to own a pen had banned her from borrowing theirs because of the terrible mauling the tips would get. Finally satisfied that what she was about to do was right she began to write in her calm controlled manner.

Two

AORO

DR AORO SIGU negotiated his way through the dense late Saturday morning traffic in an attempt to find an opening which might allow him to escape from the snarl-up in the center of the city and make his way home. It had been a hard morning and he was dog-tired. Apart from his usual stint at the clinic he had also had to go to theatre to work on a teenager who had been run over by a car while cycling and was badly smashed up.

Now in his mid-forties, he had a solid reputation as a surgeon and was at the height of his powers. He was much sought after for his unquestionable skill; but he had been going none stop for the last two years and it was time, he decided there and then, that he took a break from his patients; he would take Wandia for a much needed holiday.

His son Daniel stirred in his sleep. He usually took the ride home as an opportunity to listen to music (which he loved much to the amusement of his parents—it was so classic of Down Syndrome), or to sleep—depending on how tired he was, which he was today. He earned some pocket-money helping his daddy at the clinic on Saturdays and this had been a rather hectic day. The help consisted of nothing more than fetching and carrying and smiling at the patients waiting for his dad to attend to them, but Dan loved it. He was in his milieu in a place where all that was required of him was to do what he did best—and that was to radiate affection. At first the patients had been rather taken aback by the short awkwardly built youngster, with his slanted eyes and half open mouth, but his father looked so unapologetic, so proud of him, that they eventually not only got used to him, but missed him when he was away at his special school.

"Oh but where is Danny today?" They would ask with genuine interest.

"We need Danny to brighten up the place a bit," others would add.

"Is it dark?" Dr Sigu would sometimes ask in jest, and turning to his nurse-receptionist, "Jennifer, open up the blinds a little more, we need some light in here!"

"But you know very well what they mean Doc. Danny is a ray of sunshine on a cloudy day." Secretly he marvelled at his son's power with people.

somehow it was her approval that he sought—it was the feather without which an otherwise glittering crown would have looked sadly lacking in that jauntiness which is the spice of life. It was therefore his blessed fortune that of all women he had chosen a woman of such generosity, such an absolute incapacity for niggardliness —which was not to say that she was not tough and very demanding.

"Hi!" he answered, the fatigue falling away from him. But he noticed that her alert attention had been drawn by Danny's uncharacteristically rapid disappearance. She stopped her descent and turned to look at Danny's disappearing back.

He quickly averted his face to hide his concern. Among her many accomplishments was the capacity to read his mind, especially when he least wanted it to be read. He, however, immediately regretted this also [...] act for him and quickly lifted his face only to [...] puzzled gaze resting thoughtfully on him. He [...] on his only weapon of defence: he smiled. [...] boyish smile that had first attracted her to [...] noticed with relief that her face began to relax [...] hoped that he had bought enough time [...] whether anything serious was wrong with [...] her knowing it. [...] with being a doctor was that one died [...] deaths before the real thing appeared [...] one's agony. And now for no apparen[t] [...] ready terrified on account of his so[n]

But his father thought that the boy had looked rather exhausted of late. One had to be watchful with this particular one—at seventeen he still had very little to say for himself, and was given to lightning flus and fevers. Thankfully his childhood attack of leukaemia seemed to have been arrested once and for all, though one could never be absolutely sure where any type of cancer was concerned.

The traffic opened up a bit. Aoro made a dash for it and was soon cruising home at a good speed. Danny, who took a gleeful delight in speed and fast cars only stirred uneasily in his sleep but did not arouse himself. His father looked at him now with real concern.

This child had made him grow tremendously as a man. At first his denial had been complete and he would frequently find himself wishing that the child would simply die and be obliterated from the face of the earth—like an obscenity; a thing which should never have been or should at least have had the decency to be still-born. What value did a human being have if not in speed, action and achievement? And his wife, to his secret disgust and anguish, had doted on the drooling idiot, treating him as if he were a perfectly normal child equal in every way to his perfect siblings.

Yet Danny was a wonder-worker. How can you not love someone who treats you with constant approval; who smiled always; who never complained about the hardness of his lot? In Danny's charmed presence even hard-nuts like his twin sister Lisa and tough cookies like his brother Mugo and cousin Johnny, became fairly human. He had, with his mother ever behind him like some sword-wielding guardian angel, perhaps single-handedly forged family solidarity and generosity to a degree which would not have been possible had he never been there. He himself had grown and matured; and had come to understand what fatherhood really meant.

With his brow still creased with concern he slid the car into the garage next to Wandia's station wagon which the children had dubbed *Malkia* due to its propensity to stop in all kinds of awkward places thus necessitating urgent pleas to Mary, Queen of Heaven, for quick intervention. He then woke Danny up. The boy got out groggily and limped towards the house. Aoro cast back in his mind trying to remember if he had been limping the day before. He couldn't recall noticing it.

"Why are you limping —did you fall at school?"

"Uh uh," answered the boy shaking his head wearily, his slanted eyes lacking their usual smile. He straightened himself up trying to correct the limp with an act of the will; and from somewhere within the depths of the goodness of his heart he fetched out a smile for his father. In reality he felt like death done-up, but the capacity for discontent and complaint had been completely left out of his make up. His father persisted;

"How long have you been limping?"

"Not long."

It was a silly question, of course, for Danny lived in the ever present now. The past was forgotten and the future held neither meaning nor undue attraction. He did whatever he had to do in the now and enjoyed it in the now. His mother had once commented that this was what eternity might be like, a remark which had left her husband agape.

Danny slipped hurriedly into the house to a further questions. His father followed him only his back disappearing into his room. H uncertainly in the sitting room unsure suddenly felt so alarmed. Wandia, who m to stay at home on Saturday afternoo the stairs upon hearing her husband's

"Hi! You look tired," she said the stairs. She was in her mid-forti stunning effect on him. The beautiful women that he had and some he had even foun evocative kind of way; but had such an arresting de age, would have been the-less real attribu exactly the same the sea— inextri the wispy wo his very defi bound up with

He wallowed

Was it possible that he had come to love the boy so much—he who had loathed the very idea of being associated with a deformed child?

He remembered how as a young medic doing his Newborn Unit rotation, a baby with anencephaly had been brought into the unit. Now anencephaly is a particularly distressful malformation as the entire vault of the skull is missing leaving the brain (whatever there is of it) in full view. Usually this gives the face a peculiarly fore-shortened frog-like appearance, but this particular baby had a surprising amount of fore-brain and a perfectly developed face—a very beautiful, almost cherubic face. Aoro was fascinated and repelled at the same time. Noticing his interest, the Senior Resident mistook it for a misguided concern for the 'monster' as they called the hapless baby.

"Don't waste your time with that one. It will soon succumb to meningitis, encephalitis or simple necrotic death of brain tissues. I don't give it more than two or three days," he pronounced in superior god-like tones.

But he had reckoned without one thing—the baby's will and determination to live—even with its terrible handicap. Week one came and went. Week two likewise came and went and people began to get fidgety. There is nothing most doctors find as disturbing as a patient about whom you can do nothing, yet who refuses to bow out gracefully and quickly so that his miseries can be hidden underground, where nobody need remember them again.

The fact the baby was the first child of a young mother did not help at all. The father had taken one look and had bolted for parts unknown, but the mother hung on grimly, hounding everybody half to death with her pleas for something, anything, to be done. After all modern medicine was supposed to work wonders. She looked pathetic sitting there holding the baby, who with it's open head neatly dressed in gauze looked exactly like any other baby—in fact prettier.

Week three came and went and the mother's pleas became stringently insistent. She couldn't understand how it was that the wonders of modern medicine couldn't come up with something as simple as a cover to replace the absent skull and she would have died of shock if she had been told that antibiotics were being withheld so that bacteria could attack the exposed brain without let or hindrance; and that there had been a ferocious argument as to whether the baby should or should not be put on iron supplements to correct its anaemia. Was iron a drug or a food supplement?

The third and fourth week came and went and the baby didn't even have the grace to suffer the one hundred and one afflictions of the newly born—no, not even the normal day-three jaundice. One of the religious sisters who occasionally passed through the unit came by one evening and after conferring briefly with the mother proceeded to give the 'monster' a pretty human sounding name—Francis. That made things more difficult for to withhold care when a 'thing' acquires a human face is much harder than when the 'thing' is simply the "monster in cot 10"; and nothing humanises a person as much as having a name. A nurse found sneaking iron syrup to baby Francis was severely reprimanded.

Meanwhile his purported healers prayed fervently to whatever death-deities they believed in for the quick demise of baby Francis. Mercy-killing was not legal in the country, otherwise little Francis would have had a veritable line-up of purported healers volunteering to dispatch him to his next attempt at reincarnation. Week five came and went and Francis hung on still, by now pale as a ghost from his anaemia. He died quietly in his sleep at the age of six weeks and three days and no one could quite determine why he had chosen that precise moment to depart this world.

It was from this rather depressing experience that Aoro had acquired his distaste for the less than perfectly formed. Perhaps they were better-off dead— therapeutically aborted before being born; but then again, he could never determine even to himself whether this was truly for the benefit of the malformed or just so that the doctor would not have to face the enormity of his powerlessness on a daily basis. Dead men are after all famous for telling no tales. Dead babies are even better for they would never have had an opportunity to tell any tales.

But what do you give an aborted child in exchange for his its life, or could death be considered a gift?

Should any one person be given the power to decide whose life was worth living and whose wasn't or should the life of any human being be a radical unrevocable right, irrespective of its accidental attributes and the circumstances of its conception and birth?

Yet he himself in spite of all his medical know-how had fathered such a child and the boy had taught him the ineffable meaning of parenthood—which was to love for love's sake alone.

He went and sat down in the sofa by the window. From there he could see a riotous jacaranda spreading out its purple bed; and a poinsettia flaunting its red star-shaped blossoms at the blue sky. This year all the flowering trees, to say nothing of the shrubs, were in full bloom. He had even been surprised by the rich creamy blossoms produced by some cacti that he had never seen in flower before. All living things seemed to be in a celebratory mood. It was very beautiful and one wanted to be out of doors all the time, though Wandia's idea of a garden was not exactly what he had had in mind. A strictly groomed and trimmed garden with neat geometrically accurate flower beds would have been more in keeping with his tastes.

"But then you would have glared at the children if any of them had made the catastrophic mistake of stepping on the hallowed grass! I prefer a user-friendly garden." And indeed it was. The plants, unless they threatened to override the rights of another, rarely ever got anything more severe than the merest nudge in the right direction. The children loved it. They rolled, skipped and played ball on it. Twice a month they tended it under the direction of their mother—this included digging holes around the plants and putting in animal manure. To his amazement, the children looked forward to it.

The weather itself was as benign as only Nairobi weather could be. But today though he was staring right through it, he wasn't really seeing the glorious jacaranda or anything else in the garden. The birds of paradise could have taken to actual wing and he would not have batted an eyelid. For all intents and purposes he was momentarily blind.

Wandia finally came down and sat in her favourite place— within the crook of his arm, which, she had said many times was the only place in the whole world where she felt completely safe. Their children laughingly called it mummy's space. Of course it was also calculated to cure his grouchiest moods of which there were quite a few. It also did wonders to his self image—which generally at least doubled in size while the sessions lasted. Today it did not last very long for in spite of herself she was distracted.

"How was work today?", she asked absently moving away from him and regarding him rather gravely. He launched into a rather too enthusiastic description of the surgery of the day.

"And how was yours?" he asked trying to sound naturally interested—a loving question from a caring husband. She was quiet for a while, lost in thought. He knew that she spent Saturdays at home attending to the children and their many friends or reading in her study, but due to her silence he felt the need to repeat the question again, his voice sounding strained with the effort to sound interested. Normally, he would have let the question ride, respecting her need for silence—she loved silence and seemed to have the uncanny ability to create a kind of pool of silence around herself even in the midst of a hubbub, as if she had stepped behind an invisible curtain.

"How was your day sweetheart?" he repeated.

"Huh?" This kind of inattentiveness was so unusual from someone who normally was able to pick up the merest nuances, that he was at a loss what to say next.

"Er, I was just saying that I've had rather a hard day. I think I'll go upstairs and stretch out for a while." He got up abruptly and took the stairs two at a time. Her suspicions were by now definitely roused.

Like a tape, she played back his entrance into the house and probed it for a false note. There was his over-enthusiastic description of his day's operation; had he had a death? Usually that destroyed his day completely, but it would have been the first thing out of his mouth— he was incapable of keeping that kind of thing to himself. He hated to lose a patient. But no, he had been smiling as she came down the stairs. So what was it?

40

Then with a mother's unerring intuition she remembered Danny's retreating back. He had not come to give her his usual affectionate hug.

Her mind reeled with alarm. *Dan!*

She rushed up to his room and was not surprised to find Aoro standing by the bed. Danny was already fast asleep, a little dribble of saliva beginning to form at the corner of his mouth.

"*But what is wrong?*"

"I don't know." She regarded him with utter disbelief.

"Honestly. I noticed only today that he looked very tired and just a few minutes ago that he was limping."

"Limping?"

"Yes, limping. I asked him whether he had fallen and he said 'no', more or less—you know how Danny is. I also asked him how long he had been limping and he answered 'not long', but I don't think it is anything serious. I just wanted a little time to find out what it was without worrying you."

Wandia sat on the side of the boy's bed. With clinical efficiency, she ran her knowing hands over his body, stroking, probing, palpating. Danny woke up but offered no resistance as his mother tried to read the secrets of his body.

"Does it hurt here?"

"A little."

"And here?"

"No."

"And here?" The bone surface felt slightly thicker, nothing very determinate.

"Only when I walk."

She continued her examination a little longer, her face thoughtful. Finally she got up.

"What do you think it is?" asked Aoro.

"I am not sure, but I can see why you were concerned." To herself she thought; *how could I have been so unobservant? But he is a big boy now and largely lives his own life , as I have encouraged him to. But I should have at least noticed that something was wrong with him especially as he never complains, unlike hypochondriacs like Anwarite, who become full of histrionics at the slightest suggestion of pain. I have been careless.*

"May I rest now?" Danny broke into her thoughts.

"Yes, of course." She went into her medicine cabinet and brought him a tablet of Bruffen. He took it dutifully and turned onto his stomach. His parents were reluctant to leave his room—as if their presence alone would have warded off all evil, but no; one is born only once and thereafter must face his own destiny.

Wandia left her husband staring out of the window and went wandering around the house. There were signs of active young lives everywhere. In one room she found an old three-wheeled toy lorry that had belonged to Mugo before being handed down to Gandhi. It was smack in the middle of the floor where anyone who came running into the room and stepped on it without looking could expect to sustain at least a good sized bump on some aspect of his anatomy. There were also bits of wood, rocks and colourful pieces of paper whose use only Gandhi or young Mark could tell. She was gratified to see that there were also books on the floor, hopefully evidence that someone was at least trying to improve his mind.

The room shared by Anwarite and Ciro was in a state of almost military perfection—the beds were made, the dolls were neatly asleep in their little woven beds which Atanasi, who came from a tribe of great basket makers, had woven for the girls in exchange for labour in the kitchen. The one-eyed grey bear of indeterminate age stood at stiff and watchful attention on the chest of drawers. It had once belonged to Alicia, a gift from her long lost father. On the door was a terse statement;

Boys Keep Out!

Which was Anwarite's friendly way of telling her brothers to please stay out. Johnny's and Mugo's room was dominated by books, sports gear and a stereo set which was Johnny's pride and joy. It being such a pleasant day all the children were out somewhere, except poor Danny of course. With that thought she could no longer put off the inevitable, so she went to her study to examine her thoughts about Danny. But once there she found that she could not really think in any organised way. Instead, pictures of the boy's life from his earliest childhood kept flashing across her mind.

There, for example, was Danny at six months looking drollish, fat and happy. There he was on his way to nursery school. There flat on his bottom during a football game with his daddy and his brothers. And there was that memorable day at the Safari Park hotel where the whole family had gone to celebrate Danny's one and only academic feat—the only B he ever got in his entire academic life, never mind in what subject!

Wandia realised suddenly that she was saying goodbye to her son. Were her instincts right or was her mind playing tricks on her? Was this the end then?

THREE

DANNY

IT REQUIRED SOMETHING close to high genius to get all eleven members of so large a family together for a meal especially given the nature of both parents' profession. But Wandia insisted that, unless one was dying or was attending to someone who was, they had to present themselves for dinner every night, Monday to Sunday. Knowing how strongly she felt about meal-times with the family, her husband tried to organise his hectic schedule in such a way that he rarely missed the meal more than twice or three times a week.

Occasionally Wandia herself would be called away, but it was only rarely that both were missing in which case Alicia and Johnny presided—one calmly, the other in a gleeful chest-thumping 'you better watch out guys, if you know what is good for you,' sort of way. Among other things, he insisted on saying grace in a sonorous, unctuous tone of voice which infuriated young Gandhi to a point where he felt that he would have gladly laced his big brother's food with untraceable poison. But then all members of the Sigu family were highly independent and self-determining sort of people. Wandia had embraced the faith late but had firm and cogent ideas on how it was to be practised in her house. After the age of fifteen she appealed only to reason, but before that age you did exactly what you were told—which meant of course that Gandhi had to submit to the highest sitting authority, even if it was only Johnny.

***

ON THIS PARTICULAR SUNDAY all the places at table were taken and there was even an extra place for aunt Vera who was back on leave from the Ivory Coast where she had spent the last ten years of her life. Some of the younger children didn't know her and they studied her elegant figure and strong expressive face with interest. Gandhi, on hearing that she was an expert in electronics, was dying to buttonhole her in a distant corner for the express purpose of finding out whether she knew anything about secret weapons. She, having been driven most of her life by a passionate nature, gazed at him with affectionate understanding. She was perhaps the only living person who recognised that the energetic child had unusual strength of character and would probably go much further than his fellows if well guided. He could, of course, also end up a jailbird— there was no half-way house with Gandhi. He would live his life to the hilt.

"Bless the table, Gandhi," Wandia said, when everybody had settled down.

"Huh?" grunted Gandhi balefully, looking at his mother as if he had never heard the words 'bless the table' in his entire life. Their eyes locked. He saw a dangerous gleam in her eyes and grudgingly decided to concur. She had a look which suggested that in another millisecond she would grab him by the nape and transport him to his room where justice would be administered with dispatch to his backside. It had been known to happen, and not once either.

"Bless us o Lord and this your gift which we are about to receive from your bounty through Christ our Lord," gasped Gandhi as if he was about to drown.

"Amen," answered his siblings and elders in unison before attacking the food with healthy appetites, except for Lisa who was nervous about an exam in which she was afraid she had performed badly. In her case this most probably meant that she had not left everyone else far behind, with a practically unscaleable margin.

However, today everyone's attention was centred on Vera whom Aoro was treating with a proprietorial air as if he and he alone was responsible for the fine and impressive person his once temperamental sister had become. He could never really comprehend what it was that drove people like Vera and his dearly beloved brother Tony to do the kind of things they chose to do with their lives. But he could stand away and admire it

47

as one did an abstract painting—moved deeply without understanding exactly what it was that had caused the emotion.

Alicia looked at her with such rapt attention that Wandia smiled and looked at Vera above everyone's head. Vera wordlessly shook her head. Alicia admired Vera with a wordless devotion and had done so from the time she had been a little girl longing for a more real mother than the one she had had. Vera was not a particularly motherly looking person, but there was something about her which suggested a safe and fast harbour—someone who would know exactly what to do in the rougher moments of life. But this after all was the essence of all the world's great mothers—mothers such as the two Marys and Salome who had stood around gallows, quietly taking in the violent death of an apparent dreamer and his fantastic dream of a world ruled by love, while stout-hearted men lost courage and fled headlong into the darkest night.

Alicia who usually had little to say at table, now waxed voluble as she asked Vera all kinds of questions about her work and the countries she had been to. Vera answered her gently and intelligently, for over the years, she had learnt to treat other people's hearts and souls with delicate tact, stepping gently, but firmly, upon the threshold of that house into which not even God enters before knocking. She prayed that somewhere in the wide busy world there was a man who would be big enough to care for and heal this beautiful child, her niece.

The meal progressed without any incident worse than Gandhi loading his plate with enough food to floor a horse. His father asked him to unload some.

"But I am *hungry!*"

"I know, but we are not marooned in a desert. You can always have some more later," he answered reasonably. Gandhi opened his mouth to argue some more, caught his mother's eye and changed his mind.

Anwarite, who insisted that her proper name be used these days, tittered behind her hand. She and Gandhi never saw eye to eye about anything and rejoiced with childish glee over each other's misfortunes. Her mother glanced in her direction and she also wisely lapsed into silence.

"Lisa you have grown into such a pretty girl," Vera said looking at her. From any one else Lisa would have spluttered with fury, but Vera looked like the kind of person who only uttered what she meant. The pretty miss looked down shyly. This was a sensitive subject for she had started puberty looking like a scarecrow with a bad case of pimples. One day the kind of thing that only happens to the Lisas of this world happened to her. A boy— a huge hulk of a rugger player, the kind with a big body and not too massive head—followed Lisa home.

Everyone observed with amazed wonder as Frankenstein sidled into the house after the preoccupied Lisa who obviously was not aware that she by the sideboard even she managed to notice the tension in the room. She turned around inquisitively only to find the love-struck dolt hovering by the door.

She turned on the poor chap and let loose on him with all the pent-up fury of three years spent under the itchy torment of the healthiest crop of pimples anyone had ever seen. The boy, who had misread a distracted smile as a welcome, retreated hastily before the blazing anger of the skinny girl and slipped out the door.

"You needn't have been so rough with him," chided Wandia, "you must have given him reason to think that he was welcome."

"I did not!" the angry Lisa had sniffed before storming out of the room in utter mortification. But now everybody realised that Vera was right. Some quiet metamorphosis had taken place unobserved and Lisa had most definitely emerged as a young woman. The crop had apparently disappeared overnight without leaving a trace. Lisa whom everyone had thought too intellectual to care about her looks could not wait for supper to be over. She wanted to go and retrieve her long buried mirror for a close-up study of her restored face. She smiled broadly at Vera.

Wandia looked at Vera with unveiled admiration.

"Come on!" Vera exclaimed with some embarrassment. "I have been away for so long and I have missed you all so much that who can blame me for looking a little too closely at my nieces and nephews? And how is my Dan?", she said obviously trying to change the conversation to calmer waters. But this was definitely not aunt Vera's day. Danny, who had undergone a biopsy on a suspicious swelling found in his groin as well as a series of X-rays earlier in the day, was pushing food around on his plate, completely lost to the world. All heads swivelled in his direction. Danny remained unaware. Suddenly Vera caught the look of deep sorrow in her brother's eyes as he regarded his son. What under heaven was happening here, she wondered? Johnny, to break the painful silence that had gathered like a dark cloud, nudged his cousin gently and said,

"Danny boy, auntie's talking to you."

"Huh?" slowly he looked up. His eyes were slightly filmed as he tried to focus on her. Instinctively, Vera knew that he was dying even though no one had had the chance to tell her anything. Each person carries the dying process within himself and in some moments of acuteness one can actually hear its sounds echoing responsively to the dying call of another. Perhaps this is the reason for the passionate devotion of modern man to incredible levels of noise. It is, among other things, a means of masking out the echo of true knowledge, which might otherwise creep up on one in an unguarded moment of quiet and thus force him to look into himself—which in many instances is a truly terrifying prospect.

"I asked how you were, son," she repeated gently, her voice almost as husky as his.

"Oh, I am fine auntie," he said and then he smiled. He looked thoughtfully at her for a moment and then added, "I was thinking." He looked down at his plate again. Danny? Thinking? Danny acted; Danny lived his charmed life, but Danny engaged in thought? It was a sobering thought. But what is thought if not to occasionally leave the clamouring mind in search of true being? And that surely is not so much a function of intelligence as it is of quietude—a capacity for internal silence.

Once again the older people around the table looked at each other surreptitiously over the heads of the children.

The conversation was rather subdued thereafter even though young Mark, accustomed as he was to spirited conversation around the table, tried to make up for it single handedly. Since he insisted on feeding himself, most of his face was covered with gravy and flecks of *ugali* garnished with *sukumawiki*. Amidst his shouts and happy yells he made such a comical figure that everyone, even Danny had to laugh. The meal came to an end and Gandhi was once again asked to thank the Almighty for his largesse. Sensing the sober mood around the table he did so in an unusually recollected manner.

* * *

LATER WHEN THE CHILDREN had scattered to bed or their other occupations, Wandia, Aoro and Vera sat almost huddled together in the sitting room whose only light was now a shaded lampstand in a distant corner.

"Something's wrong with Dan, isn't there ?" Vera began. She remembered how delighted and proud she had been when her newly born nephew and niece had been shown to her, it was as if one had been given an assurance that there would be a future after all—that all was well with the world and that the universe was pleased with the race of man. Of course she knew that the concept that each person, irrespective of the accidents and circumstances of birth, was an eternal unrepeatable species complete in himself, was now almost completely alien to modern man. With genetic engineering and cloning being a likely possibility, man had become disposable. Human beings were at best treated as mere commodities to be disposed of when and as the more powerful saw fit; and at worst, as some sort of amoeba with a sexual organ—with the most extraordinary sexual latitude in human history. It was not surprising that in such a world there was no place for people like Daniel Sigu—who could only offer love, but without sex appeal. Aoro's voice struck a sad cord in the quiet night;

"I noticed that he was limping only last Saturday and when I checked I found some glands in his groin—rather large ones. It was then that his mother came in to look at him."

Wandia studied her hands and said nothing. She

had yet to come to terms with the fact that something of this magnitude could have happened once again without her having an inkling of it. She was after all an internist—used to stringing together mere suggestions into a brilliant diagnosis. Surgeons, such as her husband Aoro, were supposed to stumble onto a diagnosis only when they had laid the body open to the four winds—with the exposed offending organ trying to hide its face in shame.

And this was her baby in a way that not even little Mark, already an independent little person raring to go, was her baby. Besides when they had taken him for his preliminary tests, she had just glanced at the x-rays in passing and what she had seen was seared upon her soul with fire—the radiating spiculed blur of osteogenic sarcoma, bone cancer, on the lower end of the right thigh-bone. It looked almost pretty—like a burst of sunshine behind a cloud, but it was one of the most aggressive cancers known to man.

My poor baby, she thought, *so God gave you back to me with one hand only to take you back with the other and in this way!* By instinct rather than by studying the case (the investigations were not yet complete) she realised that this time round the prognosis would be poor, and that was why she had insisted that the boy should come home to wait for the results rather than spend a single unnecessary day in hospital. Better to be with his family than in some sterile hospital bed.

She also knew that they would soon have to face

up to the question of amputation, chemotherapy and all the other miseries of cancer treatment. Eventually she realised that Vera, who had been so close to her during that other distraught time when the boy had had blood cancer, was now looking at her with agonised tenderness. Then she came over, and putting her arms around Wandia, said to her brother,

"You make us some tea old chap. Wandia and I need to be alone for a little while." Wandia, rather irrelevantly, remembered that other cup of tea which the two of them had been having together before she had gone into unceremonious labour with the twins—Daniel and Lisa. Seventeen years ago. Where had the time gone so silently and so swiftly?

"You and I go back a long way, Vera," she said quietly leaning her weary head upon her sister-in-law.

"And that's a fact," Vera concurred. They talked quietly of inconsequential things. Of Daniel, Wandia only said;

"He never really belonged to me you know, but his was a charmed life. Part of me selfishly wants to hang on to him—how can there be a life without Daniel to teach us all wisdom?"

Vera only nodded. The two sat in silence for a while.

Aoro, looking careworn, eventually returned with the tea and an unusual bottle of beer for himself. He passed the cups to the two women then collapsed into a chair. Wandia noticed lines on his face that she had never seen before. The poor man.

Vera eventually rose to take her leave. It was very late and she knew that those with whom she was living would be anxious on her behalf. She insisted that she would find her own way out and so firm was her manner that she was out of the door before the two broken-hearted parents could react. Once outside, she stood next to her borrowed car in an uncharacteristically dejected attitude, for she was generally a clear-thinking swift-acting, kind of person. Finally, she opened the door, slid behind the wheel and eased the tiny car out of the garage into the driveway.

At this time of the night she was almost entirely alone in the streets. Even the street people, the forsaken of the earth, had apparently found some lair in which to hide for the night. Vera drove home in silence—alone with her thoughts.

She had always had a soft spot for the city of Nairobi—even in the days when the garbage mountains had been the highest on earth. The only rule on garbage collection had then apparently been—look left, look right, look left again and if no one is watching—dump the garbage wherever. The streets had been aswarm with little children hustling for coins. As for the potholes, they had ceased to be the perennial butt of the jokes of desperate Kenyans and had instead, no doubt, become responsible for many strokes, nervous breakdowns and outright death of the people, in the last years of the twentieth century.

Not that things had improved that much in this

second year of the new coalition government. Following a nerve-wracking session of general elections, during which all kinds of unpalatable human passions had come to the fore—with ballot boxes disappearing into thin air and resurfacing in distant constituencies, open bribing of voters and returning officers, to say nothing of death under suspicious circumstances of those seen to be a barrier to the acquisition of power, the first female president anywhere in Africa had been elected by a slim majority, perhaps because a critical number of people had simply had enough of the old guard and wanted a change—any change. It had also finally become clear to everyone that no single party could ever garner a clear majority, thanks to the devout conviction that one's ethnic grouping could only get a larger bite of the national cake if one's tribesmen were in power—competence and basic honesty having nothing at all to do with it.

Now the roads were a little better—not the car-eating craters of former times. And there weren't as many desperate people absolutely at their wits ends walking the streets like the damned in hell.

Still, Vera loved the city—the feel of it, the scruffy trees by the so called avenues, which most accurately reflected the spirit of Nairobi, if not the whole nation—where everyone including mothers with babies on their backs, hustled around busily, from morning till night in an attempt to make a living despite sometimes incredible odds—simply refusing to give up—like the gnarled trees covered by the grime and soot of numberless vehicles which obeyed no known laws.

She sniffed the air and then took a deep gulpy breath close on the edge of tears—for this beloved city, for Danny, for all beauty and all crushed innocence.

Yet, she reflected letting her mind rest on changeless truths as it was wont to do when she was particularly distressed, *life is a beautiful thing, a great good. This city has many wonderful people in it who are alive and have dreams for themselves, good dreams which no doubt will translate into something good for this city and this country as well. In all known human history, evil men have always appeared on the verge of final victory. But one must hope. One cannot despair.*

As for Danny, who is as innocent as the angels, and was given so little with which to pass through this life, he has done only what is good. Much is given to the rest of us but when we are not squandering it, we are busy hoarding it. No I must not despair. I must not weep.

Yet when she touched her face, it was wet with silent tears. *But who am I weeping for? Surely only partly for Danny but also partly for this world which has much to be wept for, both tears of joy and of sorrow, and partly even for myself. For is it not easy to find fault with the whole wide world yet place our own selves in the realm of the angels? I made a choice on how I would live my life, a hard choice, but I would do it again. No doubt I have done some good, perhaps even a lot of good.*

58

*If a soul is invaluable then I have been allowed to shape
the invaluable, like a jeweller. Yet even I have much to
weep for, for the times when I have caused unnecessary
pain or allowed pain that it was in my power to relieve
to continue.*

*For those moments when I have shut others out
of my heart and placed some beyond the pale, beyond
salvation, beyond hope even. For times without number
when I just did not want to know because knowing
would have meant discomfort, that I get up and do
something—get involved, and thus complicate my own
snug existence, and perhaps get hurt. How often have
I been prudent when it served my own interest, hoping
that someone else would do something before I needed
to face my own cowardice? How easy it is to find fault
with the whole world, but how hard to face the naked
unvarnished self!*

When she arrived at the house where she was
staying, everyone was asleep. She rang the bell as gently
as she could not wanting to rouse the entire house. She
was so tired she could have keeled over. It was partly
because of the lateness of the hour, partly jet lag—she
had travelled many thousands of miles only two days
before. Partly it was also due to cumulative fatigue—
she had been going nonstop for over two years.

Angels, having been named after Mary, Queen of
Angels, opened the door for her. Vera tried to arrange
her face into a calm and friendly smile, but Angels who
had been around for a while, ignored the smile when

she saw the look in Vera's eyes. She produced a thermos with the same flourish that a conjurer would produce a mouse from a hat, except that she did not say 'voila!' With an imperious solicitousness she poured out a cup of hot milk for Vera and kept her company while she drank it. Little was said, but so powerful was the sense of belonging, of being loved, of being part of something wholesome and good and even great, that a word formed itself on her lips;

"Home." Angels, who did not once attempt to pry, only nodded.

FOUR

A STUDENT DOCTOR

JOHN SIGU COURTNEY placed the palm of his right hand flat on the patient's distended abdomen and felt for the liver. It was moderately enlarged, with a hard knobbly surface. His eyes were a bleary yellow and he had scratch marks all over his body. Johnny could have rattled of a series of differential diagnoses almost effortlessly but the Examiner had picked up his confident demeanour and realising that this was a cocky and bright candidate, was out to crucify him.

"What do you know of Crigler-Najjar Syndrome?" He asked in that lackadaisical way examiners have especially when asking questions from outer space. Johnny almost yelled "*whaat!*" but somehow managed to control himself, though his mouth remained open for a moment or two. Crigler-Najjar was an extremely rare condition that Johnny was sure he would go to his grave without ever having set his eyes on, and he was almost 100% sure that the same applied to the examiner. However, he forcibly reigned in his wits and tried to recall the little he remembered of the disorder.

"It is a hereditary disease," he began haltingly, "brought about by the absence of–ur–the liver enzyme -ur–er–Glucuronyl Transferase," he paused and glanced at his torturer. He was stone faced. "There are two types," he paused again wondering whether it was Crigler-Najjar or Dubin-Johnson syndrome which had two types, then he ploughed on with desperate courage, "The less severe of the two types is responsive to Penobarbitone." He stopped because he couldn't think of any thing more to say about the confounded syndrome. To his horror the Examiner said,

"You may go."

"Wha-at?"This time Johnny couldn't help it. The word just slipped out of its own accord. Surely wasn't he going to be given a chance to vindicate himself, to answer other questions that he knew something about or at least discuss the case in front of him? He felt like weeping.

"You may go," the Examiner sounded almost gentle, but Johnny was too far gone to notice it. He turned away wordlessly with visions of repeating the year going round and round in his head. What Johnny did not realise was that the examiner had come to the wise conclusion that if you could not pin down a fourth-year-student on something as far-fetched as Crigler-

Najjar, which even many final year students had only a vague or no idea about, you were unlikely to pin him down on anything. He awarded John Courtney a distinction without a second thought.

The few days after the exams were normally given to the study of ethics and the history of medicine. Johnny loved these lectures and discussions but today attended them with an unusually heavy heart. He thought that he had flunked his exams and as if that was not enough his cousin Dan was in hospital again with bone cancer. Therefore Johnny was in a mood for combat—the kind where one unleashed one's intellect like a whiplash against some hapless person without compunction. He couldn't even bring himself to care about the fact that his teachers had the power of life and death over him, at least academically speaking. He knew they could make him repeat classes until he was a grizzled old medical student of ninety-five, but he just didn't care.

The subject matter in today's lecture was the 'declaration' that doctors were supposed to take upon graduation, since it was no longer considered necessary to take an oath. It had always annoyed Johnny—who had great integrity despite his externally care-free attitude—that the great oath of Hippocrates, which had been taken by countless medical giants of the past while being sworn into what was after all the greatest profession on earth, had been so systematically watered down as to be recognisable at all.

The watering down had begun with the Declaration of Geneva which had striven for an entirely secular approach to the oath. Johnny, to whom the Deity was very far removed in regard to the day-to-day affairs of men and regarding whom he had very many doubts, surprisingly hated the emasculated 'Declaration' passionately. He realised with unexpected understanding born of love of the science, that medicine had a great capacity for much good as well as terrible evil and those who held the power needed to swear by what they held most holy or at least what they were most afraid of.

Johnny had been surprised to discover that he distrusted men who believed in nothing but their bank accounts and who were willing to 'declare' all kinds of things they had no intention of doing. At his age Johnny had already heard of too many cases of Chronic Lucrative Appendicitis—which had nothing whatever to do with an inflamed appendix, but everything to do with a doctor's financial well-being. Johnny felt that even though money was very important, life was most important. Once he had recovered from his childhood malaise and depression, Johnny revelled in his own life, enjoying the grace and power and beauty of his mind and body. One could not have lived with Professor Wandia Sigu without coming to accept the utter dignity of the human person;

"Even the street urchins?" Anwarite had once asked in disbelief and much to everyone's amusement.

"Most especially the street children whose plight automatically diminishes the dignity common to the race of man. Man is advanced enough to walk on the moon, but not enough to feed his brothers on earth at a fraction of the cost or better still share with them the know-how. Despite all the hype and propaganda, this world has the capacity to feed us all with plenty to spare. Actually, I think it pure arrogance for this generation to imagine that it has exhausted all discoveries in regard to the production of food and human health or anything else for that matter. We have barely scratched the surface of the earth. Great and amazing breakthroughs are yet to be made. We must never confuse science with politics and human greed. The problem is not the carrying capacity of the world, it is the hoarding capacity of its people." The older children who understood the innuendo, burst out laughing. Anwarite remained puzzled, while Gandhi, in his favourite tattered shorts and ancient baggy tee-shirt, whose colour defied all description, looked like just a slightly cleaner version of a street child.

So, as fate would have it this day, Johnny sauntered in with the other students and took his accustomed place in the middle of the lecture theatre. Everything was all right until the lecturer, Dr Gara, a young rather unscrupulous physician, decided to make a scathingly dismissive statement concerning the Hippocratic Oath.

"Before a young doctor is let loose upon the unsuspecting populace, it is necessary for him to at least give assurance that he won't do too much damage. But of course it is no longer necessary to swear to the kind of sonorous nonsense that doctors had to pretend to believe in in bygone days. We are an emancipated profession with different values these days. The Hippocratic oath is a useless anachronism from a bygone era of superstition and ignorance. We appeal only to science." It sounded very polished to everyone else but Johnny.

Now medical history was his particular hobby—he found tracing the development of medicine from the early masters who had had so little to go on but their wits, to modern microsurgery, very rewarding. And of all the scintillating stars who had ever blazed their way through the medical firmament, Hippocrates, born 460 years before Christ and living to a ripe old age of 83 to practice the art, was his favourite. He considered the Hippocratic Oath a masterpiece expressing in lines of extraordinary beauty the true nobility of medicine and its practitioners, now lost in a utilitarian world. Also he did not consider the lecturer worthy of any kind of emulation. As far as Johnny, who had accompanied him in several medical rounds, was concerned, he was an incompetent medical thug, the kind who still existed only because Hippocrates had been dead these many thousands of years. Johnny raised his hand slowly and the class, who recognised his belligerent stance, groaned because they realised that they were unlikely to leave the class on time. Nobody cared very much one way or another —oath or no oath.

"Sir," began Johnny in so well-mannered a voice that even his aunt Wandia would have approved of it. "Please explain to us why the Hippocratic oath is a useless anachronism from a bygone era of superstition and ignorance."

"Come on, Courtney, what do you expect from an oath that begins by invoking a bunch of gods and goddesses, and anyway who needs to take an oath nowadays? The Declaration of Professional Dedication is good enough." He coughed with false politeness but real impatience.

However, for Johnny, mention of this declaration was like holding a red flag to a bull. It was one of the bastard offspring of the Declaration of Geneva, which, when all was said and done, had at least some semblance of professional dignity in it. As far as Johnny was concerned, the Declaration of Professional Dedication consisted of a series of spineless platitudes that left out anything that might disturb the conscience of a modern day doctor, no longer only a healer and preserver of life, but a dispenser of various kinds of death as well.

Dr Gara grabbed a copy of the Hippocratic Oath, regarded it with an amused smile and waved it to the class.

"Listen to this," he said sardonically and started to read the opening lines of the oath:

I swear by Apollo, the physician, and Aesculapius and Hygea and all-heal (Panacea), and all the gods and goddesses that, according to my ability and judgement, I will keep this oath and stipulation.

"What the hell is one supposed to make of this kind of crap!" he interjected, but went on reading without allowing anyone a chance to say anything.

"To reckon him who taught me this Art equally dear to me as my parents, to share my substance with him and to relieve his necessities if required; to look upon his offspring on the same footing as my own brothers, and to teach them this Art if they shall wish to learn it, without fee or stipulation.

"By precept, lecture and every other mode of instruction I will impart my knowledge of the Art, to my own sons and those of my teachers and to disciples bound by stipulation and oath according to the law of medicine, but to none others...

"What old fashioned nonsense!" With this second interjection, Johnny could not take it any more.

"What's so old-fashioned about respecting your teachers and colleagues?" he shouted derisively. "I should have thought..."

"Shut up Johnny and let us hear..." Mwikali Nzomo tried to interject hoping that Dr Gara would get over with it.

Dr Gara ignored them and continued over the din starting to rise in the class:

"I will follow that system of regimen which according to my ability, I consider for the benefit of my patients and abstain from whatever is deleterious

and mischievous. I will give no deadly medicine to any one if asked, nor suggest such counsel: and in like manner I will not give to a woman a pessary to produce an abortion.

"With purity and holiness I will pass my life and practice my Art. I will not cut a person who is suffering with a stone, but will leave this to be done by men who are practitioners of this work. At this point Gara issued an expletive that set the class roaring with laughter. Johnny's protest was swallowed in the noise and he fumed silently waiting for another chance.

"Into whatever houses I enter I will go into them for the benefit of the sick and will abstain from every voluntary act of mischief and corruption; and further from the seduction of females or males, freemen or slaves.

"Whatever in connection with my professional practice, or not in connection with it, I may see or hear in the lives of men which ought not be spoken abroad, I will not divulge, as reckoning that all such should be kept secret.

"While I continue to keep this oath unviolated may it be granted me to enjoy life and the practice of the Art, respected by all men at all times, but, should I trespass and violate this oath, may the reverse be my lot." Gara paused dramatically and again before Johnny could get over his anger and say whatever words choked in his throat, concluded:

"Hippocrates did live to a great old age and no

doubt enjoyed his life thoroughly, but I think that this was because of his excellent constitution and not because of this quasi-religious stuff," he concluded with a cynical smile.

"On the other hand," Gara said, ignoring the few raised hands "the Declaration of Geneva adopted by the World Medical Association in 1948 is only a slight improvement on Hippocrates, but at least they don't confuse medicine with religion. Listen to this and compare." He picked another copy from his table and began to read in a monotone:

"At the time of being admitted as a member of the medical profession I solemnly pledge myself to consecrate my life to the service of humanity. I will give to my teachers the respect and gratitude which is their due. I will practice my profession with conscience and dignity. I will respect the secrets which are confided to me, even after the patient has died. I will maintain by all means in my power the honour and the noble traditions of the medical profession. My colleagues will be my brothers. I will not permit considerations of religion , nationality, race, party politics or social standing to intervene in my duty to my patient.

" I will maintain the utmost respect for human life from the time of conception. Even under threat I will not use my medical knowledge contrary to the laws of humanity. I make these promises freely and upon my honour."

"Not too bad, but the best of them all as far as I

am concerned, and the one which best reflects the aspirations of a modern doctor, is the Declaration Of Professional Dedication which succinctly states:

I solemnly promise to practice the Art of medicine with due care and conduct becoming a physician. In the exercise of my profession I will ever have in mind the care of the sick and the well-being of the healthy. In the furtherance of these ends I will use all my knowledge and will strive to perfect my judgement. I will furthermore keep silence on any matters I may witness or hear in the course of my professional work which it would be improper for me to divulge.

"I promise as a graduate in medicine, that I will promote the welfare and maintain the reputation of the medical profession. I will also accept my responsibility to pass on the knowledge I have gained and recognise my debt to my preceptors."

Gara paused to let them take in the wisdom of his declaration and Johnny finally grabbed the chance.

"Actually," said Johnny in a deceptively mild voice, "I'd imagine that if a person is going to do things like open me up and delve around my exposed insides or shoot up powerful drugs into my system or even give me all kinds of potent stuff to take orally, then I'd feel much better if he swore by something much bigger than himself, that he would at least try to do his best to maintain my life to the best of his ability, and that he would not allow the temptation to make quick money override his judgement, especially if I happen to be an inconvenience for someone. Of course, woe to me if the only thing he believed in was his bank account; in that case I suppose a declaration of dedication would be better than nothing."

The students laughed uproariously more to get rid of their post-exam tension than anything else, but also because the man was well known for his avarice. The lecturer glared balefully at Courtney as he gathered up his papers. He would probably find ways of crucifying Courtney, but that was Courtney's problem. After all he should have realised by now that the maxim for survival in medical school was to keep your mouth shut. It never did do to take on a lecturer—they were a hypersensitive lot to say the least.

Mwikali Nzomo raised her hand. She was a very tall girl with one of the best minds in the class.

"I don't believe in any of these declarations. I think a doctor is the best person to decide what is good for her patient, and the patient herself of course, if she is competent. As for this whole business about respect for human life, I believe that every woman has the right to choose what to do with a pregnancy which she herself is carrying. It is she who stands to lose. The doctor is there only to assist her get what she wants, a live birth or an abortion. The doctor is not there to moralise anybody!"

Several hands shot up at once followed by several voices. The situation got completely out of hand as the students yelled all kinds of things at each other;

"You Courtney! You male chauvinist pig!"

"If your mother thought like that you would never have been born, Mwikali, and good riddance!"

"Witch! The baby has a right to be born!"

"Down with declarations!"

"Down with exams! I'm sick of them!"

Gara rapped sharply on the table with his pointer to get some attention. He had had enough of the silly brats, besides he was late for a case—money called.

"For your home-work," he said as a passing shot, "I want you to write an essay comparing the merits and demerits of the various oaths and declarations that doctors have found it necessary to bind themselves with since the Art and Science of healing began; and also whether there is any need to continue this nonsense in the twenty-first century and if you think so to formulate a declaration which according to you would be fitting and give reasons why you think it is most appropriate." With that he stormed out—leaving the students groaning for never before had they been given any homework in an Ethics class. Nobody believed in all that stuff anyway—the economic reality out there was simply too harsh for any person who wanted to live comfortably to allow medical ethics to get in his way in any big way.

***

EVEN AS SHE MADE her way down the dimly lit hospital corridor Wandia realised that she had not come to a decision about whether to accept amputation

73

to be done on Danny's leg or not. Though the tumour had already spread to the lymph nodes in the groin and probably in the abdomen, the lungs still looked tumour free and removing the primary focus of malignant activity would enable the boy's doctors to battle the cancer with chemotherapy. It would at least give him a fighting chance. But surgery of such magnitude would take its toll and chemotherapy, with the highly poisonous methotrexate as the mainstay of treatment, was pure murder. She was tempted to just quietly let him go, but she knew she could not. Who knows but that he might be lucky this second time round too. And everybody loved Danny so much. There was no way his siblings would accept that he be left to die without being given at least a chance. Besides he had beaten the odds once, hadn't he?

She turned a corner and entered the Adult Oncology ward where Danny was sharing a partially partitioned room with a boy in his early twenties who had an AIDS related Kaposi's sarcoma—usually a slow growing cancer of the elderly, but in the case of AIDS patients, an aggressive and rapidly fatal disease. The boy, to put it mildly, was terrified and distraught, unable to even begin to understand the terrible things that were happening to him. He spent hours staring into empty space and every once in a while would raise his voice into an incredulous moan,

"But I am only twenty-three!" As if death and dying ever only happened to decrepit old men of a hundred

74

and twenty-three. He had been brought up in a world of instant gratification and did not therefore have the moral or mental resources to see him through his predicament with at least a modicum of human dignity. No one had prepared him for the inevitability of the fact that actions had consequences.

Finally Danny, recognising a soul in utter agony, had gone over to sit with and hold the hand of the shuddering youth. It was in this posture that Wandia found her son. The boy had fallen into a sorrowful and exhausted sleep and Danny smiled wanly at his mother,

"He was so sad, mama."

Wandia helped Danny arrange the boy in his bed and then Danny limped to his side of the room and sat down heavily on his own bed. Wandia, regarding her son with pride, thought to herself, *'and wisdom, disregarding the clever, has found refuge in the simple.'* She decided that such a man, for this was no longer a boy—definitely not like the one in the other bed—would fight gallantly to the end. If this thing could be beaten, then Danny would beat it. She sat down to explain to him about amputation. It wasn't easy for either of them mainly because the boy did not have the words to ask the one or two questions on his mind or the words with which to console his mother who was obviously suffering so much. Finally he just said,

"It's okay, mama, Danny is a big boy now, mama," whereupon Professor Wandia Sigu, strong and intelligent woman of the world and no stranger to tragedy, rose and went to look for a toilet in which to shed her tears.

When she came out, the boy's father, his aunt Vera, Johnny, Lisa, Alicia, Mugo and Anwarite were around the bed. Gandhi, Ciro and little Mark had been barred from entering hospital premises due to their age—a state of affairs which left Gandhi so furious that his speech sounded as if he was speaking in tongues. The tight circle turned around expectantly when they got a glimpse of her emerging from the bathroom. The decision to amputate was simply too big for anyone but her to take.

Aoro's face was a study in suffering. In his heart he felt that God, if he really existed, should have spared him this great misery, he who had brought so much relief to so many other people. Wandia who knew him almost better than he knew himself, realised that this crisis had just brought to a head things that he had never really allowed himself to face before. She had always marvelled at his capacity to survive by refusing to scratch anything but the merest surface of things. She thought that he, a brilliant man, had allowed his thought-process to ossify and to become redundant. It made her feel both sad and guilty for she loved him deeply.

"Danny and I have discussed this," she said in an uncharacteristically abrupt voice. "He understands. Your father and I will go to sister's office to sign the consent form immediately." Without another word she

76

turned on her heels and started off down the disinfected and sterile white corridor.

"*A place without a soul,*" she thought and was surprised at her sudden spirit of dissatisfaction and rebellion—she who had spent most of her adult life plying these or similar passageways where modern healers did daily battle with inexorable death. Ashamed of her momentary capitulation to weakness she stopped and waited for her bewildered husband to catch up with her. She tried to remember that he was a better man than most and that this was not his fault. As he caught up with her, she looked into his eyes and could not help thinking again, "*he suffers like an animal—without hope or even understanding —I really have an obligation to outlive him, how could he face his own demise alone?*" She placed her hand into his square capable one and noticed that the palms were wet.

"Don't worry so much," she urged him. "If any one of us is going to be all right, it is Danny."

"So you think the prognosis is good?" he said, eagerly wanting to clutch at any straw. She was quite taken aback at being so thoroughly misunderstood and only just managed to stop herself from saying something that would wound him enough to wake him up once and for all.

"One must always hope," she said instead, remembering something that the beloved Father Tony, his brother, had once said;

"Kill a man if you must but never deprive him of hope—for with that you kill him anyway and in a much more cruel way." Tony. She must call him as soon as possible. Sometimes she thought a bit irreverently that Jesus must have been like him—spreading hope and goodness and love in places where one would never have thought that such things could exist, like the lust-possessed soul of the Magdalene or the withered little heart of short Zaccheus who had been in love only with money until Jesus came along to fish him out of a sycamore tree.

She hated to disturb him—he was so busy, but this was a family emergency and his brother needed him. Apart from looking after a busy parish in one of the toughest areas of the city, he lectured in philosophy at both the University of Nairobi and the Catholic University. How he had made those arrangements no one knew, but he had always insisted that he also needed to do parish work if only to save his own soul.

"The halls of academia are a veritable jungle of pride and jealousy, my dear sister," he had once said to Wandia whom he would occasionally engage in animated discussion. "Christianity is a religion which demands simplicity of heart, but how truly hard it is to be simple in the midst of the back-stabbing and glory-seeking which is the perpetual curse of the world of learning and the learned."

"But surely, a priest defending a doctorate in philosophy or theology, can hardly be the same as someone defending a doctorate in something purely secular?" Wandia had countered, but not really too surprised.

"On the contrary, pride is the pitfall every person striving for excellence must deal with. One's state in life has little to do with it."

And I also need him, she thought suddenly, *my nerves are completely shattered, I need to hear Tony's healing words. And soon Aoro and I must go for that much needed holiday. We both need it badly.*

Being a full time professional and the parent of a large family had its satisfaction and its drawbacks. One of the more chronic drawbacks was the sheer scantiness of time, especially time for things like holidays and relaxation. But on the other hand there was the incredible satisfaction and highly enriching experience of having brought into existence such a wide, not to say wild variety of human beings. No single day was monotonous. No day was like the ones that had gone before it. One was constantly kept on tiptoe.

There were the days when one was likely to be called in by revered educationists to answer charges in regard to one Lwanga Gandhi Sigu, a person named after a modern day African saint and an Indian statesman and hero, but whose un-saintlike activities might cover anything from mere misdemeanours, to felony, and even to high treason—such as placing a rubber snake on the teacher's chair and causing the worthy gentleman to leap in undignified fear, for which crime the little felon had suffered a whole Saturday morning in detention. And for the days when one was called to view the almost too perfect work and behaviour of one Anwarite Sigu whose progress and behaviour were strictly according to the textbook. Or for the terrors of being the mother of such a one as Lisa Sigu whose future was uncertain in spite of her mighty brain.

Her friends and neighbours had long since given up trying to understand why an intelligent woman of the world might want to have six children even without the spectre of Down Syndrome hanging over one. However, one could not browbeat her with accusations of ignorance—her professional prestige was impregnable and who could know more about the techniques of avoiding or annihilating a pregnancy than a doctor? Also her house was always open to her children's friends; nobody felt superfluous in that house, everyone, whatever their foibles, was treated as if they mattered— as if they were important.

And so, every weekend youngsters, escaping from the gloomy elegance of their own homes and, to the amazement of their parents who pandered to their every whim, wandered off to take a whiff of the bracing air of the Sigu household—where they were often seen working with their hands, *their own hands!* in the garden or at the kitchen sink, or at some other menial task which they had never been known to perform at home.

The matter of going away for a while had become a serious necessity and could not be put off for too long any more. It would probably be best when Johnny and Alicia were in recess. Between the two of them and with some help from Lisa and Mugo and highly competent house-help in the guise of Atanasi, the cook and Sabina his wife who also doubled up as the maid, they could surely manage for at least ten days. Danny's hospitalisation was of course the deciding factor, but as soon as he was better and at home, or whatever eventually awaited....

FIVE

I SWEAR BY APOLLO THE PHYSICIAN

AFTER DINNER THAT NIGHT Johnny asked his aunt whether she would help him with an assignment. She pretended to gape at him.

"Of course! I am highly honoured. How long has it been since you last asked? Close to a decade?"

"It is serious, auntie. Besides I fear I have worsened my already endangered state by taking a lecturer head-on."

"That sounds pretty serious, son. Haven't I often warned you to leave some of these pompous asses well alone? Who was it this time?"

"Well, it was Dr Gara and he was going on about the Hippocratic oath."

"The Hippocratic oath! That's a good one. How did it come about?"

"Actually, that's not it exactly. But Dr Gara did say that the Hippocratic oath was a useless anachronism of a by-gone era of superstition and ignorance, to quote him exactly."

"But why?" Wandia asked, puzzled by the vehemence of the statement, but, of course, Gara stood unchallenged in the area of pomposity and self-importance. Most doctors tended to respect other colleagues, alive or deceased, if only in recognition of the fact that the science was built on both the advances and mistakes of the past. After all, once upon a time, the only known anaesthesia was a glass of whisky and a blow to the head to knock the patient senseless before the surgeon could get down to the grissly business of sawing off a limb. One just had to respect doctors— even the African medicine men of the past who had made holes in the heads of their patients to let out the pressure (and the evil spirits). The mortality could not have been too great as the practice had continued sporadically well up to the end of the twentieth century —especially in instances where western medicine was perceived to have failed.

"Well, one of the reasons he gave was that the oath began by appealing to a bunch of gods and goddesses."

"But I thought you didn't believe in them either or even in God as understood by the monotheistic religions of the world."

By this time the rest of the family, sensing that an interesting discussion was about to take place, had drawn near, no doubt to participate in the true Sigu spirit of vociferous and passionate conviction—all except Aoro who was still lost in sad thought.

"You misjudge me, auntie. I believe in the principle of the thing—"

"What thing?" asked his aunt mercilessly.

"That there is some sort of Supernatural Intelligence out there but nobody can really tell what he is up to—except perhaps that he is intelligent and therefore knows the difference between good and evil, right and wrong and, and—" He stopped, feeling awkward and a bit foolish.

All eyes were regarding him with rapt attention—after all he was the family's avowed atheist or so Mugo had thought until today. Mugo was still at the point of vacillation—atheist, agnostic and firm believer—especially when he wanted the Almighty, in the guise of his parents, to provide something he badly wanted. In spite of this he had admired his cousin as a brave man of conviction and therefore worthy of emulation at some later date, when he, Mugo, had fewer needs to be met and hopefully less need of the Almighty's intervention. But what was this about a Supernatural Intelligence? Did it mean that even tough Johnny believed that God existed? Interesting thought!

"And?" urged Wandia.

"And that he punishes the evil." Wandia felt like laughing outright except that she recognised Johnny's youthful and passionate idealism.

"If that is your reason for believing, then you ignore the evidence of your eyes. The evil *do* prosper. Take Dr Gara— he drives the kind of car your uncle and I would have to work for a hundred years to afford, and his home is marbled practically to the front gate —not of course that I have any proof but that he practises only clean and dedicated medicine." Johnny snorted in profound and utter disbelief, and everyone laughed.

"Actually what I meant was that medicine is too noble, too endowed with a capacity for both great good and terrible evil, to go into without at least appealing to something bigger and holier than yourself and your bank balance." OK. There it was. He had said it. They could laugh if they wanted to, but that was how he felt. But no-one laughed— least of all Wandia. She could have mentioned the Hab theory just to confound him and his inconsistencies.

But she more than anyone recognised that in every person's life there had to be a moment of insight and personal revelation. Perhaps it came through a sick child as it had been for her. Or the death of the beloved. Or the play of a ray of sunshine upon a patch of grass. Or the invigorating smell of air after it had been washed clean by a storm. Or to an aspiring healer of disease ridden and broken human bodies searching for some honesty and truth—as it was now for Johnny. But how quickly the stray thought is put away lest it drive away complacency!

She looked up and saw that her husband was looking at his nephew rather fixedly. But he said nothing.

"So what was the conclusion?" Wandia asked, turning to Johnny again.

"There was none. Dr Gara thought that something called the Declaration of Professional Dedication was good enough for a modern doctor who believes only in science, such as we are supposed to be."

"Since when did we do away with the Declaration Of Geneva?"

"I don't know, auntie. But since I sounded a bit unimpressed by all these declarations, anyway, and the class laughed rather uproariously—er, at some of the things I said, we were all given the assignment of writing a fitting declaration."

Wandia laughed at that.

"That sounds original." But Dr Gara was not exactly famous for originality of thought. "You must have incensed him thoroughly."

"Actually, I was already put off by the clinical exam —I had a really terrible examiner. I think I flunked my clinicals and you know that if one fails the clinicals nothing can save you, not even a 100% score in the theory."

"Well, you know that medicine, like carpentry, is an apprenticeship, and even if you write brilliantly about how to make a table, if you make a crooked table, you are a lousy carpenter. And people value their lives more than they value their furniture."

"But this chap asked me about the Crigler-Najjar Syndrome!"

Wandia laughed at the look on Johnny's face.

"The examiner has the right to ask you anything he likes so long as it is a known medical condition."

"I agree Auntie. Actually I didn't mind the question as much as the fact that he wouldn't ask me other questions. I felt cheated. After all I had prepared very well for this exam." *And no doubt you were dying for a chance to show off!* thought his aunt knowingly, but she only said,

"Oh well, examiners know what is best." Johnny could have argued the point, but decided to get back to his assignment.

"So how do I begin my oath?," he wailed.

"Well, I agree with Dr Gara that one cannot begin by declaring allegiance to gods that no-one believes in any longer." This came from an unexpected quarter. Lisa had previously left no one in doubt as to her lack of interest in medicine.

"OK! But does one take an oath or merely declare their good intentions? Doesn't an oath bind you in some way? And if that is the case what does one swear by?"

"Well you could swear by Almighty God," offered Mugo just to test the waters.

"But not every one believes in him or agrees about his nature," countered Johnny.

"And even if they did, who would make them do what they promised?" asked Anwarite, surprising everyone by this insight into the real difficulty of the matter. But then she had a healthy suspicion of the intentions of most human beings anyway.

"I suggest," said Aoro coming out of his deep

reverie. He had been thinking of his dying son alone in the huge lonely hospital where even as of this moment someone who had lost the battle for life was no doubt gasping his last. He reached for the copy of the Hippocratic Oath that Johnny had been waving around all this time and started to scan it. He said again, "I suggest that it might sound something like this:

"I swear by all that I hold Sacred and dear, and by the Noble Profession to which I have been called, and recognising the great contribution to the art of healing by men and women now gone; that according to my ability and judgement, I will live in accordance to this oath_"

Warming up to the subject, he went on:

"To hold my teachers in utmost esteem and to endeavour to pass on the knowledge and skills acquired in my lifetime to the next generation of those aspiring to the profession—without holding anything back.

In caring for the sick, I will use only regimens which I consider of most benefit to the patient while trying with all skill to minimise any harmful effects they may have. I will shun adventurous medicine whose sole purpose would be self aggrandisement. I will not wilfully bring about the end of a patient's life under any pretext either by withholding appropriate treatment or by administering deadly drugs, neither will I obliterate life after conception or in-utero for in such weakness and vulnerability do all men, small and great, begin their lives. I am a healer and therefore called to enhance life where possible, but never to destroy it.

I will struggle always to ensure that my intentions in regard to the sick are pure and that my personal life is exemplary, for men look up to me as one granted great power—the power of healing.

I will not use my favoured position for purposes of seduction of the patient neither will I divulge any knowledge acquired in the course of my profession unless it is for professional reasons or for the good of the patient.

If I live in accordance with these tenets which my noble forbearers have held true, then may I prosper and grow in understanding and skill. On the contrary if I allow greed or pressure to blind me or move me from my way, then may I suffer from both legal and natural justice from which no man can ultimately escape."

Dr Aoro Sigu stopped and the silence that ensued was unearthly. Nobody had ever thought him to be imaginative let alone creative. Johnny looked at him as if Hippocrates, that worthy medical gentleman, had come back to life after almost two thousand five hundred years of repose.

Another revelation, thought Wandia in silent wonder. The other children regarded this suddenly unknown father with solemn eyes and then wandered off to their rooms to try and understand.

***

AND AT THE HOSPITAL Danny whiled away the pain and the long night hours praying for his family—

little prayers that Wandia had taught him. And he told Jesus little secrets that only Danny and Jesus could understand.

The doctors had already started him on a course of chemotherapy to shrink the tumour and to determine its responsiveness to anti-cancer drugs. He appeared to respond well so they went ahead and amputated the limb and this was uneventful. They continued to bombard his system with three powerful drugs one of which was so poisonous that he had to be rescued with the vitamin folic acid, every 24 hours after receiving it or else he would have died. It began to look like he would pull through and so he was encouraged to start learning how to use crutches. It was his priest uncle, Fr. Anthony Sigu and his cousin Johnny, who was almost a doctor himself, who seemed to inspire the boy most during that difficult time. Danny's disability made him anything but dexterous—in fact at the best of times he was awkward to the extreme. And now he had only one leg to work with!

"Try just once more old chap. Think how happy your mother will be if you learn how to do it." Fr. Tony would whisper in his ear. But before Danny could really get the hang of it the Doctors had to flatten him out again with another course of powerful drugs. Nobody knew where or how he got the time, but the priest spent two hours of every afternoon with the sick boy. He was there during the miserable retching and nausea that nothing could really control.

The boy and the man talked for hours in low voices— nobody knew about what. Danny—who had never talked much in his entire life. Sometimes, on days when he was not too badly off, people could even hear him laughing in his low hoarse voice at some of the things Fr. Tony said to him.

"But what do you talk to him about?" his brother Aoro asked him once.

"It is not often given to men to consort with angels, old chap, or to see the face of God daily." Was Tony's ambiguous reply. He did not really expect to be understood, but was surprised to see his brother nodding his head in what appeared to be actual understanding. Suddenly he remembered how the two of them had been inseparable as children and how much they still loved each other despite their markedly different lifestyles.

"It's going to be all right," he said, putting his arm around this wounded parent, his brother. Once again he was surprised at the serenity of the answer,

"I know."

Johnny on the other hand brought the ailing boy a rakish red cap with the name of a famous soccer team on it to cover his head when his hair fell off in great big patches. Danny loved that cap and went to all his therapy sessions with it. He became a thin, wan figure, the only spot of colour being the bright cap on his bald head. Whenever possible, Johnny personally came to give Danny his intravenous drugs. He felt that his familiar hands were more soothing than a stranger's would be. When Danny wasn't too sick he also told him all kinds of crazy stories that he made up on the spot and which made Danny weep with laughter.

Johnny also tried to befriend the boy with AIDS. There was something about the destructive terminality of the disease that fascinated him. The inexorable ravaging of the human body which nothing could really stop even after years of research, left Johnny with a gut-sick, helpless feeling. There was also the terrible stigma. AIDS was the leprosy of modern times. Johnny would go over to encourage the youngster, but he was so psychologically battered that he despaired of reaching him.

"Come on old chap, you can't just give up without a fight. You can get on top of this thing. Please Try!" Johnny would urge. He identified closely with the boy who was practically his age and was taking a degree in architecture. It could be him lying there with a terminal illness! The boy's formerly doting parents were completely shattered and hardly ever came to see him.

"But I'm dying! Don't you understand? I have AIDS!" groaned the boy, whose name was Andrew Karama.

"Listen, Andy. The truth is we are all dying, the only question is when. But why should death find you lying down and waiting? Why should you die a minute before you absolutely have to? *Me*, I have promised myself that death will find me on the run and will have to work damned hard to get me. Come on! You must graduate and at least put up some buildings!"

"You are crazy," said the boy but some light came into his eyes.

After a few days, Johnny found him with his hair combed. He was also surrounded with books.

"That's the spirit, Andy!"

"Thanks, Johnny." A long lasting friendship was thus born.

Danny was approaching the final leg of his treatment when his blood count suddenly plummeted to a haemoglobin level of a mere three grammes. His platelets, essential for blood clotting, practically disappeared from his peripheral blood, and he started to haemorrhage from every orifice. They gave him endless units of fresh blood and eventually arrested both the anaemia and the bleeding, but soon after this the boy went down with a raging pneumonia. The bacteria raged through his weakened lungs without let or hindrance, solidifying and digging cavities in the tissues. Wandia noticed that the boy offered little resistance and she was tempted to urge him to fight back, but then Danny opened his slanted eyes and gazed at her with such love and peace that she could not speak at all.

He died soon after; rather he slipped away quietly and nobody could detain him. It was a long time before his parents and Fr. Tony, who had come to administer the last rites, could bring themselves to move away from his bedside and to let go of this treasure that had graced their lives for seventeen charmed years.

"May the angels meet you at the gates of paradise," declaimed Fr. Anthony Sigu in solemn respect for the dead and death.

"Amen," echoed the two who had given Danny life.

They took Danny Sigu and laid him to rest alongside his grandparents at the farm in Njoro. He had borne a great ancestral name and so his simple memorial plaque read:

DANIEL ODERO SIGU
Dearly beloved son of Wandia and Aoro
You changed our lives.

SIX

JOHN

WITH A PRACTISED pilot's eye, John Courtney studied the screen where the progress of the Royal Dutch Airline plane was being charted. The plane had just crossed the Blue Nile to enter South Western Ethiopia from the Sudan and it would be at least two and a half hours before it landed at the Jomo Kenyatta Airport in Nairobi. He had been flying, or waiting around in airports, for the last fifteen hours and he was exhausted; but that did not prevent the surge of adrenaline in his blood when he remembered how much he had loved this land and the beautiful woman who had made him want to make it his home.

He had loved her perhaps more than one should love another human being, with his entire being. But in his heart he had suspected that she really did not belong to him or to anyone else for that matter. She was one of those people who belonged entirely to themselves, for the simple reason that they could, apparently, only love one person and that person was basically their own self.

Without bitterness, he could still remember the pain of her betrayal and the casual way in which it had been done, but nothing could really justify the way he had abandoned his children. He had wanted to come— oh how often he had wanted to come, especially when he had heard that she had died, and in such a terrible way too. But somehow his relationship with her had left him feeling like a maimed bird— with only one wing and therefore unable to fly.

Finally he had met another woman, Sybil Stanley— an artist. Sybil did not have the wild and exotic beauty of Becky, but she was an incredible person in her own right. She had helped him patch up his wounded soul— effectively, but with a kind of cool detachment which, in retrospect, had proved more healing than a more maudlin sentiment would have been. For her sake, but more so for his, he had tried to close the African chapter of his life. He put away, but could never bring himself to destroy the photograph of himself, Becky and the children, taken just before the break-up. He and Sybil now had a ten-year-old daughter, Andrea, upon whom he poured paternal affection. He had done his best to forget the other two haunting faces.

And he thought he had, until Wandia, that wonderful woman, wrote to him again—a letter which had cut through the hardened scar tissue over his heart with one swift stroke.

96

Dear John,

I hope with all my heart that this letter finds you (it had, even though he had changed his address several times and there was no logical reason why the letter shouldn't have been lost completely somewhere along the way). *We are all very well minus the chilly political winds that blow across this continent every once in a while. I hope that the years have dulled your pain a little bit, because the time has come for you to take care of some of your unfinished business. I have tried to the best of my ability to care for your son and daughter and they have turned out into two very fine people. I love them very much, as does their uncle, but though you have tried to play dead, they know that you, their true father, are alive. And if you are alive then the only interpretation they can put on your behaviour is that you have rejected them, and for reasons which are beneath contempt—such as their mixed race.*

I really cannot go on defending your behaviour for ever, so come or make sure that someone sends us an authentic death certificate, the kind you get when they bury you six feet underground and place a large slab of marble on top to make sure you don't change your mind and try to dig your way back to the surface.

Even though we never met I still consider myself your sister-in-law because here in Africa, relationships are not deleted just because a judge says so, so I hope that you will take all this in a brotherly spirit.

Affectionately, Wandia

Some years back he had received his first letter from Wandia which had read,

Dear John,

We have never met, but I am married to Aoro, the late Becky's brother. No doubt Vera has been keeping in touch with you and has told you that it is Aoro and I who have been looking after Johnny and Alicia since the death of their mother. I just wanted to let you know that they are doing very well and that Johnny wants to study medicine. Even though both my husband and myself are doctors, I felt that you may want Johnny to do something different, say flying. After all you are his father and he may want to follow your footsteps. Why don't you write to him— he would be delighted to hear from you. If you need to know anything else about them just write to me.

  Better still why don't you pay us a visit?

Sincerely, Wandia.

Due to a great, almost pathological inertia, John had done nothing after receiving that first letter. Besides he was afraid to interfere in another person's life after

98

having been away for so long and he thought that not only was he superfluous, but would be told so to his face.

But when he read her second letter John felt so deep a sorrow that he wept, with a terrible heaving sound—the way men who have never found easy recourse in tears, weep. It brought Sybil running from her studio—where she spent each afternoon creating breathtaking pieces of modern art with things that appeared like bits of odds and ends—to John at least. He agreed that they were beautiful, but could never understand why people, to say nothing of galleries and museums, trampled all over each other for a chance to buy her works, and at sums which were indecent to mention in polite society.

It was apparently John's fate to meet women who were preoccupied with something else. In Becky's case the something else had been her extraordinary beauty and her exaggerated sexuality which was in essence just a preoccupation with her ego, her unadulterated love of self. On the contrary Sybil was pre-occupied only with her art and not even her child was allowed to interfere with her hours of creativity which demanded intense concentration. Her work was so evocative that the interplay of light and shadow suggested intricate movement, like a dance motion caught in an instant of time. It required immense concentration. But this was in her case the precise reason why she could love John in a way undemanding enough for him to get the time and space he needed to heal. She understood that one could love at different levels and even in different ways, yet love honestly and deeply.

Sybil had even seen the hidden photograph with the stunning looking woman and her lovely children, and artist to the core, her only reaction had been—*a black Venus! Someone should have painted her*. She knew that the time would come when he would talk to her about it of his own accord, but she would do nothing to precipitate it—she did not *need* to know, but she would be there for him if he ever needed to be heard.

She picked the letter from his unresisting hand and read it. She then put her sensitive artist's fingers at the nape of his neck and massaged it until the heaving ceased. And then the words and the pain spilled out of him, and with them the putrid poison of years of suppressed bitterness. At the end of it all, he became aware of the nature of the touch of her hand and his own crept up to it and the two entwined, speaking to each other the language of love and of hope and of new beginnings.

"You will have to go and see the children, if you can call them that. Try to bring them back with you if they are willing. I would love to meet them."

John looked into her eyes and then looked away. There was a word that was used for the kind of man who has a treasure in his hand but does not know it. If he remembered correctly the word was idiot.

"I've been an idiot, but I want you to know that I

love you very much and I don't deserve you at all." She laughed and her lovely grey eyes danced with humour. And John, for the life of him, could not remember seeing them like that before. He felt like a man coming to the end of a long, long journey.

So here he was flying KLM to Nairobi, excited and afraid at the same time. Why had he waited so long? What was he hoping to salvage this late? But as Wandia put it—it was unfinished business. He should have come when the kids were still little. Especially when Becky died. He should have taken them with him—or could there have been some truth in the fact that he would have felt uncomfortable raising two coloured children by himself? Marrying across racial lines tended to put one's personal integrity in question—not of course that he had exactly been a tower of respectability before. Was that what he had been afraid of then? He cast back in his mind and he could only remember the dark pain. She had not been the first woman in his life, but she had been the first woman he had loved completely, even blindly which, he was beginning to realise, was perhaps not a good way to love. She had been blindingly lovely and a blinded person is never in a good position to judge. But again didn't they say that it was better to have loved and lost than never to have loved at all? And of course he now had Sybil whom he had taken for granted far too long, he had a lot to make up to her for.

He must have dozed off because the next thing he

heard was the professionally confident voice of Captain Johannes van der Meer warning the passengers to fasten their seatbelts as landing was imminent. John righted his seat and watched with amused interest as a mother did battle with her active three-year-old who simply would not sit still long enough to be fastened into his seat. Eventually throwing diplomacy and decorum to the four winds, she simply manhandled him into his seat and pinning him down with her upper arm, she succeeded in connecting his seat belt.

The child opened his mouth and yelled, more for effect than in the hope of securing release. Sensing complete and utter defeat, he eventually subsided and glared around pouting. John smiled at him and nodded. The boy regarded him with interest and then smiled, but the plane took an alarming dip and he turned to clutch at his long suffering mother.

John looked out the window and saw, with a quickening heart rate, the wide tan sweep of the Savanna beneath him. How often he himself had taken his own plane through that approach, expertly losing altitude and banking it for a landing so soft that it frequently drew a round of applause from the passengers. It had been a long time since he had last flown an airliner, but he still remembered those long hauls across oceans and continents with nostalgia. When Captain van der Meer finally brought the great big bird down, it was with such a feather-like lightness that John could find no fault with it. There was the inevitable round of applause from relieved passengers. It was after all human nature to feel truly safe only in *terra firma*—despite the truly incredible numbers of people who daily took wing to crisscross the planet.

As he checked himself out, he saw that the once spic and span Jomo Kenyatta Airport was much the worse for wear even though there was evidence of an attempt at a face-lift. He wondered whether there was anyone to meet him and how he would know them. Perhaps they would have his name on a piece of cardboard, or perhaps Aoro, his erstwhile brother-in-law would remember him. He doubted whether he could reciprocate; it had been around a decade and a half since he last saw him—a rather cocky medical student in those days.

But when he walked out into the waiting area he recognised the trio instantly—his son, his daughter and, no doubt about it, Wandia—looking exactly as he thought she would, calm and collected, medium height, good face, thoughtful intelligent eyes but somewhat dreamy and interiorised. Wandia and Alicia saw an older replica of Johnny and Johnny saw his reflection, but with silver hair and a care-worn face; and rather sad eyes.

The four moved towards each other as if drawn by a magnet, then Wandia drew back a little not wanting to be in the way of the reunion. Johnny in his turn hesitated. It was Alicia who went forward and threw herself into her father's arms like a waif come home;

and John thought with a stab of pain—*Oh my God it is Becky all over again !* But then again it wasn't; this girl had a sensitive mouth and incredible eyes. And tears started unbidden from his eyes and his heart moved within him, a lurching sensation, as if the moorings had been torn off. And Johnny, seeing the tears, almost forgave him. They shook hands in a rather formal way, looked into each others eyes and decided to risk a bear hug. They both survived it and turned to Wandia.

"You must be Wandia." Between two infinite moments, he had changed from a tired and anxious looking elderly man to a very charming and good looking one. "As you can see I am not dead yet." Wandia had the grace to look a bit embarrassed at his reminder of the contents of her letter. Then she laughed in her open friendly way.

"Welcome, I'm so glad to see you. Yes, I must say you look pretty much alive."

"What's this business about being alive?" asked Johnny suspiciously.

"It's a secret between your father and myself." He looked at them curiously and wondered when and where the two had had time to share a secret.

"Aoro was unable to come —he was called away at the last minute."

"Must be pretty busy, mustn't he?"

"Quite, but there are bad days and good days."

John turned to his son:

"So I hear you want to be a doctor too." Johnny's

eyes turned defensive and something alarmingly hostile leapt out of them. John realised that he had to be very wary with this one. "I was delighted of course. If I remember correctly, there have been healers on you mother's side from time immemorial. It's in the blood." The hostility left Johnny's eyes. He smiled and nodded his head lightly. And his father remembered that to the African, blood was something tangible and real, a communal identity much more powerful than the mere biological liquid.

With wisdom born of suffering he realised that the African identity was something that was not only important to his son, but was in fact what had given him stability in what must have been very turbulent formative years. It was only understandable—it could not have been easy growing up with an almost white face and no real parent to even show for it. John suffered another stab of guilt and turned to his daughter. He saw from the way she gazed at him that all she had ever really wanted was to have her daddy with her and therefore as far as she was concerned the past could be erased with that generosity that only women are truly capable of.

"And you my girl, what it is that you do?"

"I study music and I teach it, daddy." That word—daddy. It hurt him rather to hear it. It was as if she was still his little girl running after him on the day he had finally left Becky.

"Daddy, daddy, don't go, daaadddyy—!" For she had

been old enough to understand that basically she had only one parent. Her mother had been too preoccupied with her own perfection to pay too much attention to a child—once the basics such as being born were over. Of course the children were scrupulously clean and well dressed, but somebody else had been paid to do it. Alicia had known about the other men, for she had seen them, and had suffered the way only a child can suffer, labouring as it does under vague fears and dark foreboding, without any real understanding of the motives and terrors of the world of adults.

Johnny studied his sister with interest and decided that though he himself could put up with the idea of a father, he was not about to allow him to dismantle his life. It was simply too late for that sort of thing. But Johnny also had the intelligence to realise that showing up this late must have taken a great deal of courage. He would start from that and just call John *father*. Daddy was a bit too saccharine for him. He didn't even know the chap, for heaven's sake! In reality Johnny's heart was full of unresolved contradictions and bitter anger just waiting for an inopportune moment to explode. He was a walking time bomb.

The tight little group headed for *Malkia* which made a few asthmatic sounds of protest before allowing Wandia Sigu to head it down the highway back to the city. John watched with amazed and very concerned interest as she expertly manoeuvred the snarling station wagon through the streets of Nairobi which were filled with drivers who apparently were all out on some sort of suicidal mission. Johnny looked at his father's face and then remarked, laughing;

"I'm afraid auntie learned driving in the days when we were living in the Eastlands of Nairobi where some of the toughest drivers on the planet live. She had to survive somehow. In fact some of my most vivid childhood memories are those of her spirited exchange with matatu touts whenever the earlier versions of *Malkia* ground to a halt between two threatening matatus."

John, who had already been introduced to the current *Malkia*, asked to be enlightened as to the nature of the matatu.

"Well," said Alicia, tongue in cheek, "they are modes of public transport which operate outside all laws known to or made by man including the law of gravity."

"Anybody has a problem with my driving?" asked Wandia as she moved into a narrow slot between two cars in the next lane—which appeared to be moving infinitesimally faster than the lane they were on.

"Nooo!" came the chorus from the back-seat drivers. No one wanted to distract her attention even for a second.

Finally, as they left the city center for that part of the western suburbs which had inspired the name of Spring Valley, John saw that the Sigus must have long since left Eastlands behind them. Wandia drove into a driveway at the end of which stood a spacious house, built along very simple, clean lines. John remarked,

"What a lovely place!" It was true. The house lacked the contorted overstatement characteristic of its neighbours. And it was set in a lovely garden at the corner of which was a rocky cactus patch which was Wandia's pride and joy. There were all kinds of rare cactuses in it. Aoro had wanted to build a home for the woman he loved, and left to his own devices, he would have gone on a flight of fancy that would have far surpassed the efforts of his neighbours, but Wandia had kept a firm and restraining hand on him and the builders.

"I don't want a mausoleum," she had stated in no uncertain terms. "I want the kind of place the kids can run around in without getting a guilt complex." However, Aoro had fought tooth and nail for the retention of a magnificent marble fireplace which Wandia considered an eyesore, but which was a source of great satisfaction to him. He frequently stood in front of it rubbing his hands vigorously even when it was hot and there was no fire.

He had insisted on calling the house *Villa Wandia*, much to the chagrin of his wife. But in this he had been vocally supported by the children, and outnumbered, Wandia had had to acquiesce. However it was strange how frequently *Malkia*, with Wandia at the wheel, found cause to make contact with the little signboard by the gate which bore the legend *Villa Wandia*. Finally, in complete exasperation, Aoro had had it embedded in the concrete of the gate post, out of reach of the car and its driver. It was not as visible as it had been before, but it was not a perfect world now, was it?

Somehow in spite of the ten souls already in residence, they managed to fit John in, though an old bunkbed had to be reconstructed and placed in Johnny's room so that Mugo and Gandhi could move back in with him. Mugo had moved to the room which had previously been shared by Danny and Gandhi thus leaving Johnny to graduate to a room by himself.

***

It was Gandhi, who, missing Danny so much, told John about his death.

"Did you know my brother Danny?" Gandhi announced in his artless manner. "He was my best friend and we used to sleep together in your room now. I don't like Mugo very much. He teases me."

"And where's Danny?" asked John innocently.

"He went to heaven."

"Oh!" John could think of nothing else to say for a while.

"But when?"

Gandhi hemmed and hawed but couldn't quite come up with the date. Finally he dashed to the kitchen and asked his mother,

"Mom! When did Danny go to heaven?"

"Who wants to know?"

"Uncle John!"

"Tell him that Danny went to heaven on the 5th of July." Though John could clearly hear the conversation through the open kitchen door, Gandhi, who was an original if ever there was one, dashed back into the sitting room and told him the date of Danny's demise in tones loud enough to enlighten the deaf. No doubt there had been many 5ths of July since time began, but the last one was only three weeks ago. Could it be? But John was too embarrassed to ask especially for fear of the manner in which Gandhi might repeat it. Nobody behaved as if there had been a family loss not too long ago. He had been welcomed into the bosom of the family with an authentic joy, not at all overcast with shadows.

Finally Wandia emerged from the kitchen and John asked his question as gently as he could;

"Oh, Danny died only three weeks ago." She turned away swiftly to arrange some articles on a sideboard which obviously did not need arranging, but not before he saw the tears spring to her eyes. A raw wound he should have left well alone.

"I am truly sorry," he said lamely, feeling like a blundering and insensitive idiot. He owed a lot to this woman. When she felt more composed she turned to him and laughed a little.

"Danny was a wonderful person to have around, we all loved him. He made us all better than we actually were."

110

She brought John a framed photograph of Danny and he saw the slanted far set eyes, the low set ears and the partially open mouth and concluded the obvious. He looked at Wandia inquisitively not trusting himself to speak. She accurately read his mind.

"Yes, Danny had Down Syndrome." But then she realised that Danny was not a phenomenon that could be truly explained. So she smiled somewhat enigmatically at John Courtney and changed the subject.

***

JOHN SPENT AS MUCH TIME with his children as they would let him, which was fairly easy with Alicia as she was equally eager to get to know her father. Johnny, who had been named after his father in better days, was a different kind of person altogether. For one thing, apart from the hectic demands of med school, he had a busy social life. Secondly he just did not seem interested in fostering the relationship. He had only a vague memory of his mother and no one had ever had the heart to tell him what had torn apart his family so early in his life. All that he really knew was that his mummy had died and that his father had left them to be cared for by relatives.

It is easy to forgive the dead, but over the years his attitude toward his father had soured and hardened. It was okay that the guy had eventually turned up, it helped him understand better who he was, but he really did not want to get close to him that much. Why bother when the chap would no doubt arise sooner or later and return to wherever he had come from, and who knew how long it would take him this time to remember that he had left his children behind? What did he really care? *In any case I myself am a grown man. I don't need anybody.*

One day his sister cornered him on his way out and looking pained, asked him why he was giving their father such a rough time.

"Why don't you give him a chance? Everyone makes mistakes and besides mum, I mean our real mother, gave him a really hard time of it."

"And I am held responsible for their differences? What was their problem anyway?" But Alicia shied away from the question. Some things could never be uttered out loud. Let the dead rest in peace. Not being a person capable of guile, she ineptly changed the subject and immediately wished that she had kept her mouth shut.

"Has dad told you that we have a sister?"

"No doubt white," was Johnny's rejoinder and Alicia's heart quivered at the look in his eyes and the way he said it.

"Ye-es," she stammered. "Yes of course. Her mother's white."

"I now understand why he suffered such total amnesia," spat out Johnny with pure venom.

"You don't understand anything at all, you self-centered idiot," Alicia yelled at his retreating back in uncharacteristic anger. "You think that you are God's answer to mankind. That you are just too wonderful. Let me tell you—the mistakes *you* will make will make you squirm in misery. And dad's errors will pale into insignificance when compared with the suffering *you* will cause." Johnny stopped in his tracks and turned around just as John who had been snoozing unseen, in a corner of the garden, and who had heard every word of the exchange, rushed up. He placed gentle arms around his trembling and by now weeping daughter, and looked with sorrow, with deep parental pain and regret, at his son.

Johnny returned the look in confused agitation. He shook his head as if in a dream then turned and walked away.

Never in the twenty-three years of his life had his sister raised her voice at him, and to accuse him of such unspeakable things! As if he had ever been cruel or proud; he was quite a nice guy, wasn't he? But he hesitated in mid-step, looked as if he might turn back then walked away shaking his head as if it was full of cobwebs.

Father and daughter returned to the spot where John had been sitting before, behind a thick and rather tall cluster of bird-of-paradise flowers—poised for flight with their orange wings and purple hearts. Before the commotion he had been gazing at the flowers and thinking what a wonderful mimic nature was. So excellent was the idea of flight that it had to be repeated in still form and vibrant colours.

He sat on the rather uncomfortable garden chair while Alicia preferred to perch on the grass at his feet, her head resting near his knee. They sat like that for a long time each lost in thought. Then John sighed and said in defeated tones;

"He will never forgive me."

"He will too. Just give him time."

"Do you think he will agree to come and visit us in Canada?"

"I would be most surprised if he did not, that would require an almost superhuman will, which I can assure you he does not have, strong willed though he is."

"Would *you* ever consider migrating to Canada?" John dared to ask, his breath bated.

Alicia was again silent. For a long time. So long that John started to chide himself for pushing his luck too far. He was going to alienate her as well as her brother.

Alicia's eyes travelled thoughtfully around the garden where each plant was allowed to express something of it's own peculiar nature. *Just like Wandia*, thought Alicia, tears springing to her eyes.

"For a long time after you left and mum died I felt quite frozen. I could feel nothing. I wanted to go and live with Aunt Vera whom I admired very much, but I could not for a number of understandable reasons. Unfortunately all I saw with my child's eyes was another rejection. Then aunt Wandia came along."

114

John nodded understandingly.

"She is an incredible person."

"I've only recently come to realise how much I love her. If I ever have children, I pray that I will be half as good a mother to them as she has been to me." She paused for another lengthy period and then went on, "I love this country. It is my home as no other place on earth can ever be." John felt that he had to say something even if it might shake up the fledgling relationship a bit.

"You *are* Canadian too and Canada is a beautiful place, though I must say the weather is not as benign as it is here. And you would love Brampton which is quite near Toronto but far enough from the hustle and bustle of that giant city to make a difference. And the suburb we live in is very nice too." John cleared his throat and plunged on, "And I am certain that you and Sybil would get along quite well. And Andrea would be delighted to have a big sister."

Alicia had doubts regarding this latter assertion. It was probably mere wishful thinking on John's part. Andrea would probably feel exactly as Johnny felt about the whole business of having strange brothers and sisters sprung on you when you least expected it, and to make it worse she was an only child. But she only said,

"I *know* daddy. I am looking forward to the visit, I really am."

What a good sport she is, thought John Courtney.

"Do you think you might broach the subject of coming to Canada with Johnny."

"No way!" Alicia said laughing. "That, daddy, is your personal cross."

John continued sitting in the garden for a while longer trying to make up his mind how to approach his son. He was occasionally tempted to despair, to simply give up and take his more willing daughter with him, but he realised that he had come too far to give up. He accepted that a showdown with Johnny was inevitable, the boy was boiling for it.

He tried to work out several ideas on how to bring about the showdown; he toyed with the idea of taking the boy out for a drink, but cringed at the very idea of making a spectacle of himself in a public place; besides he didn't know the boy's drinking habits at all. He could just imagine a drunken Johnny yelling the truth, the whole truth and nothing but the truth at him, while the other patrons glared or hissed at them.

In the end he could not really think of any viable solution so he got up and went into the house to rouse up a conversation with that rascal Gandhi, but he only found young Mark and had to content himself with his endless questions.

"*Unco*, why are you so white?"

"Because the colour got finished before God painted me up." And invariably there would follow fits of delighted giggles. A delightful child, Mark.

SEVEN

FATHER AND SON

JOHN SIGU COURTNEY, despite his worst fears, passed his exams near the top of his class. As he told his family the good news he rubbed his hands gleefully together, a mannerism he had picked up from his uncle. His father, John, beamed at him proudly from across the room,

"Congrats son!" It was a spontaneous, unpremeditated commendation, therefore it hurt much more than it would normally have when the boy didn't even look his way. Johnny ignored him totally. He acted as if he had heard nothing. Wandia glared at him wishing that he was still of an age at which things could be done to his bottom. Johnny, feeling on top of the world, her also. Aoro only looked at him sadly, embarrassed on John's behalf.

"Your father said something," Wandia said, her voice rasping with anger, the words hardly audible. "You could at least thank him. I don't recognise you, Johnny."

"Oh yea? Thanks *father*, but where were you all those years when uncle and auntie here sat with me late while I finished my home-work? Where were you while they worried themselves sick whether I would turn out okay? Where were you on those nights when auntie spent sleepless nights worrying about my childhood illnesses? Where were you while the other kids taunted me, calling me *whitey,* and I could have polished my face with black shoe polish? *Where the hell were you!"*

Both his aunt and uncle moved towards him, as if to restrain him, so furiously had he attacked his father. His feelings were much worse and much deeper than even they had suspected. But John's calm voice sailed across the room,

"I believe John and I need to talk man to man. Please leave us alone," he said refusing to use his son's diminutive, but smiling at Wandia and Aoro. Astute Wandia however noticed that his eyes were clouded and remote from the hurt Johnny had inflicted so mercilessly on him. *A good man who has been hurt once too many,* she thought, her heart welling with compassion for him. She had never before really accepted or understood that John could have received an almost mortal blow from his late wife. This Sybil must be a very good person to have helped him heal so well. She suddenly realised that it was most probably because of Sybil that he had finally gathered the courage to come. Some people love so completely with their hearts that their whole being becomes maimed if that love is betrayed.

John Courtney was one of those unfortunate people. At the beginning the children would have been a constant and unbearable reminder of what might have been but never really was. In any case it must have taken at least an unusual degree of courage for him to spurn culture, heritage, ethnicity and inbred prejudice, to take an African woman for a wife despite her legendary beauty. Aoro had told her with a mixture of amusement and amazement that the man had even taken the requisite dowry to the father of the girl. Old Mark Sigu had been too flabbergasted to know what to do with either the animals or the man except to try and accept gracefully, like a dyed-in-the-wool African patriarch would have done. He had been most disappointed with his daughter's conduct and the breakdown of the marriage, though in all honesty one could never have expected too much from that girl. All she ever had was on the surface only, there had been something twisted within her, which was rather terrible considering her angelic face.

Aoro put his arm around her reluctant shoulders and gently dragged her out of the room. When all was said and done, Johnny was her baby as much as any of the others and she had a maternal fear of allowing anyone a free hand with him without her being there to gauge whether the justice being meted out to the child was not also heavily weighted with mercy and understanding.

When the two were alone the older man cleared

his voice and began to speak in a low voice. Johnny continued to stand belligerently in the middle of the room, but as his father went on, his shoulders relaxed and he collapsed in the nearest chair his head held in his hand as if it was too heavy for him.

"I loved your mother very much. You must have heard that she was an extremely beautiful woman, she made a man feel as if someone had grabbed him by the throat, but that was not the reason why I loved her so much, though everyone assumed that it was. In some ways she had a childlike innocence and I found the combination irresistible. I wanted to possess her and care for her and protect her, like an expensive and rare object, all very manly feelings but of course these days manly feelings are rather suspect—someone might just accuse you of being a male chauvinist.

"She looked very helpless—like a child. But children, precisely because of their undeveloped innocence are capable of great cruelty as you yourself have experienced. I don't know whether this has been expounded in any religious book, but sometimes I think that one needs to suffer the consequences of evil before one can even begin to understand what evil is.

"But your mother lived somewhere so far from the surface of her being that she was completely untouched by the pain of evil. And she never emerged long enough from it to really reach out to anyone at all not even to you, her own children. She was therefore capable of being cruel in an incredibly careless way as if she was unaware of the hurt she was inflicting, like a cat scratching, like a child stabbing. *But I loved her.*

"I could have competed with the other man in her life, if it had been one man, but there were several. She really didn't seem to care who she ended up with. Yet I am sure even now that if she ever loved anybody at all, it was me. At least enough to have two children with me. Eventually I did the only thing I could do, I left. Everyone believed that it was I who divorced her, but I didn't have the strength or the desire. How do you divorce a little child for hurting you? But in the end I think she just hated my guts. She worked out all the technicalities and just informed me that it had been done, and that she had full custody of the children. Just like that. I suppose I could have fought, but apart from anything else we were continents apart. I was flying around the world pretty regularly then and I was away from home frequently. Unlike here, we don't have an extended family to call upon when things get rough. My only living parent was in an old people's home.

"When I finally got your aunt Vera's letter informing me that your mother had died—,"

Johnny broke in and asked a question whose answer had eluded him over the years,

"What did she die of anyway?"

John looked at him in amazement.

"Don't you know?"

"I don't, despite asking several times."

At least one bit of bad news that they left for me to

break! John marvelled at the Sigu's capacity to keep a secret.

"She died of AIDS, one of the first casualties," he said. And after all those years he could still feel her suffering pouring into his heart like an invisible wave of pain from a dark past.

"Oh!" Johnny said in a small voice. They sat in silence for a while, sharing the companionable pain.

"They wrote and told me that you and your sister were living with your uncle and aunt. I was shattered, but I really couldn't think what to do. It can happen that a man can become completely numb, completely unable to plan. And I was living such a nomadic life that I felt that perhaps it was better for you to live with a family that was intact.

I can see now that I was utterly mistaken and I am sorry. But I can't change the past. I can't be there to see your six-year-old face as you open your birthday present, or be there to hear about your day at school, or to hold you when you feel that things have been too rough. I am much the poorer for having missed these things, and don't for a moment think that the fact that I have another wife and a daughter makes it easier. No child can replace another. Each child is unique as is the relationship between the parent and that child. I know that you may not believe it and with good reason, but I love you son and I have thought of you often and prayed for you. Believe me when I tell you that even the most atheistic parent is a firm believer where a child is concerned.

"Johnny, if you could only give me half a chance, I believe that we could at least work on being friends now. None of us can choose our parents and for a damn good reason—the great majority of parents would be left childless, most have feet of clay, are bad tempered, cowardly, weak, disorganised, the lot. Johnny, I may not be much and I know I have caused you a lot of pain. But I am your father, the only one you will ever have, and that is not to belittle your uncle or aunt and the absolutely wonderful job they have done with you. As a matter of fact I think that they are among the few exceptional parents that many children would freely choose. No wonder they have so many—there must be a veritable crowd of children up there clamouring to be let into this family—"

Johnny smiled at the picture the older man was drawing. It did his father good to see that smile. It was simple, amused, unguarded—a boy's normal smile lacking its usual brittle, cynical twist when speaking to his father.

"Come on son, I would appreciate it from the bottom of my heart if you would come and spend sometime in Canada with me, in my house, as my son. I am not asking you to leave Kenya forever. But I need to get to know you and I think you need to get to know me." Johnny looked at his father for a moment and then shook his head.

"I am afraid," he said simply.

"But of what, son?"

"Why did you come after so long?" Johnny prevaricated not wanting to discuss his many nameless fears.

"Your aunt wrote to me about you and I felt that truly if I was still needed after so long an absence, I should not waste another minute. Sybil, your stepmother that is, felt the same."

"Won't she mind having us there? After all she doesn't know us."

"She will be delighted, I assure you she can't wait."

"And what of the little girl?"

"Ah Andrea! I assure you John, you will love Andrea. And she will absolutely adore having you with us. When I called them yesterday, she asked me how far away Africa was since it was taking so long to bring you home."

Johnny laughed at that.

"Africa *can* be quite far," he concurred. "In any case I can't just leave without discussing this with uncle Aoro and aunt Wandia."

"By all means, old chap. Listen, I have no intention of making you sever your relationships here. I think they are all wonderful people and I could not have chosen anyone better to take care of you kids when you were little; who knows, maybe they have done a better job of it than I would have done. But life is a matter of growing and part of growth is having the courage to forge new relationships."

"You are beginning to sound like my aunt Wandia—she is quite the philosopher."

There was a thoughtful silence. Johnny was somewhat surprised that his father was a man whom it was very easy to be with, a man one could like or even admire. He was steady—affectionate without being stifling. And he was confident—a quality John could admire and even identify with. One could imagine his steady hands on the controls of a plane with the lives of hundreds of people relying on his skill and ability. *Why, I wouldn't mind being like him!* Johnny was very surprised to discover this longing within himself—it felt like a total capitulation, but again he didn't mind. *He is my father,* Johnny thought and realised that this was a turning point for him. Finally he gave body to his thought, "Do you know, when I was very little, well not so little—about ten or something, I wanted to be a flying doctor, the kind of doctor who takes help to the most out of reach patient, who otherwise would die unattended. There are still many people in this country who live way out of reach of any kind of medical care."

John looked at him quizzically, a smile lurking in the depths of his eyes.

"Well, what's preventing a bright young man like yourself with lots of brains, confidence and a supportive family from doing exactly what you feel you should do?"

"Nothing." Johnny mumbled in his throat as if he were still a little boy, not really wanting to be heard. *After all a man had to have some pride, bwana!*, he thought to himself.

Then almost as an after-thought he added, "Would

you teach me how to fly, dad?" That word again, *dad!* John could not help it, unobtrusively, he hugged himself —it felt so good to be a father, and of a lad such as this.

Why, he thought with profound surprise and some sorrow, which is something that almost always accompanies a deep personal revelation and self knowledge, *I am a fatherly person, I am only now truly revealed to myself as I contemplate myself in this other, to whose existence I have so essentially contributed, who is a continuation of myself yet is not me. He makes me feel that I have not lived in vain. I am a father! And this, seated near me, is the evidence.* He wanted to share this new self-realisation with Sybil, but Sybil was not only thoroughly modern, but profoundly Canadian. He had grave doubts if she would fall in with his discovery that being a father was the greatest thing that could happen to a man, at least not to the point of giving the theory flesh and then carrying it herself for nine months. *But I have to make her understand, for if being a father is so deeply significant how absolutely elemental is motherhood, not just the biological act, but the deep meaning and connection and essence of carrying a living being within you, nurturing its body and spirit.* Still there was the nine months and the labour, to say nothing of wakeful nights and endless worries. *But she is an intelligent woman, she will understand what it is I am trying to say. She is deep. I shall appeal to that depth.* John was so surprised at his trend of thought that he chuckled to himself. *I am becoming a real philosopher!*

He was silent for so long that Johnny was afraid that he had been rejected yet once again.

"Oh well, it's not very important."

"Of course it is!" John said snapping out of his thoughts. "It is very important. I'd be delighted to teach you. Let's go out to Wilson Airport tomorrow and see what they have to offer. I might even find a retired buddy or two still holed up there. And then when you come out to Canada, we'll do even more than that, OK?"

"That's great!" Johnny answered, his handsome face wreathed in smiles.

He then got up and went in search of his uncle and aunt.

***

HE FOUND THEM in the back balcony with young Mark, Anwarite and Ciro. Anwarite was reading a book with her usual supercilious air. Mark as usual was holding center stage with all kinds of fantastic questions only an almost-three-year-old mind could think of. He had an exceptionally extensive vocabulary for his age. Today, Ciro, who was still close enough in age not to find his inquisitiveness irritating, was answering as reasonably as possible, questions ranging from why shadows follow people around to why couldn't the cat learn how to talk.

"Because he is a cat. Cats can't talk," Ciro said.

"Besides *you* talk enough for ten cats and at least

three small boys," his mother added.

"Do I?" asked the young man, quite delighted.

"Yes," insisted his mother. "Imagine what a terrible noise there would be if the cat also started asking as many questions as you do!" She started mimicking. *"Miaow? Why do little boys talk all the time?"* Mark found the prospect so amusing that he collapsed in a fit of giggles just as Johnny joined them.

"Jon-jon," squealed Mark from the floor. "Have you ever heard a cat talking?"

"Well, that depends," Johnny answered cautiously, not knowing what had transpired and not wanting to blow up somebody else's tall tale.

"Mum, show him, show him!"

"No, I will do nothing of the sort! And it's time for your nap!"

Mark protested this as a matter of form. He rightly suspected that naps had been invented for the welfare of grown-ups not of little boys, so he went to his father and asked to see his watch. Aoro pulled up his sleeve and exposed his Seiko for Mark's scrutiny. After carefully studying the face of the watch Mark grudgingly went to lie down in his cot. Exactly three minutes later he was fast asleep. Mark, of course, could neither read nor write let alone tell time, but he liked to impress upon everyone else that he had a mind of his own.

"Auntie, uncle, I wanted to talk to you, "John said, his voice sounding strange.

Wandia studied his face for a little while and then

128

asked Ciro and Anwarite to leave.

"But why?" asked Anwarite, speaking for the first time. The balcony was a pleasant place to sit and it was made pleasanter by the fact that both parents were available.

"Johnny wants to talk to us." Aoro answered seeing the impatience on Wandia's face.

"We don't mind," Anwarite answered, acting daft.

"*Please!*" Wandia snapped in no uncertain terms.

"OK OK!" Both girls rose and made their departure. Johnny tentatively sat on the chair that had been vacated by Anwarite.

"My father–er–dad and I have been talking," he began sheepishly.

His uncle leaned forward encouragingly, his supple surgeon's hands intertwined together. However, neither he nor Wandia uttered a word. They let Johnny feel his way around the words he needed to use. In a way this was a catharsis for the boy, a definitive turning away from the shackles of the past.

"He invited me—" again he stopped and looked thoughtful. Wandia's maternal instinct was to reach out and ease out things for him, say something that would make him understand that he was well understood, but again she desisted realising that Johnny needed to get many things off his chest.

"I want you to know," he finally blurted out, "that you two are the best parents a guy could wish for, that in my heart when I think of the word parent you will come first to mind. Not once did I ever feel that I was anything but part of the family, that I was not only loved but only the very best was expected of me and for me. Not once were you afraid to demand from me. It is only now that I begin to realise that this is not something to take for granted. To raise someone else's child well, whose parent furthermore is known to be alive and who might turn up to make demands, cannot be easy. And God knows I was never the easiest of children."

That, Wandia thought, *was the understatement of the year*. Johnny's reminiscence made her remember just how tough it had been, especially at the beginning. The boy had arrived practically bereft of the power of speech. Then he had gone through ferocious temper tantrums that shook his small skinny body with dumb fury, and during which one could only leave him alone until his anger had spent itself leaving his body limp like a rag doll. Then, though everyone assured his aunt that he was a very intelligent child, he went through a whole year without opening his mouth and appeared to learn nothing. His only participation in school activity consisted in fighting boys twice his size—the smaller ones were scared to death of him.

He would come home with a broken lip, a split brow and a rapidly closing eye almost every day. It was a question of loving the unlovable and the thankless, but his aunt tried. He never wanted to be touched by anybody, but she would sit by his bed and just hold his little hand which was all the contact he would allow.

My God, please don't let him grow up to be another Tyson!– Tyson had gone down in history as the ferocious boxer who bit off another boxer's ear in a bout of ring frenzy.

Twice a week she took him for therapy, where he demonstrated time and again the desperate anger of an inchoate mind, but otherwise he didn't seem to make any progress.

Then one day after a particularly ferocious fight in which Johnny got two black eyes, a puffy lip and multiple bruises, and it transpired that he had fought three older boys, two of whom had had to receive stitches, his desperate aunt bathed his bruises and, at her wits end, started talking out loud to him.

"You are a handsome and intelligent boy Johnny, and I love you very much. You see, you are my oldest son and Danny and Mugo look up to you. All the boys in this family will want to be like you one day. And that makes me so happy because I know that you will grow up to be a wonderful person, a person who cares for people and who works hard in everything he does."

Johnny looked at his crazy aunt out of the chink left in one of his swollen eyes. Hadn't he just fought three of the toughest bullies in his class and didn't he plan to go and clear up another two as soon as he felt better? He was *tough* and he didn't need anybody.

Yet surprised out of his wits, he croaked,

"You think so?"

"Yes of course, I never say anything I don't think."

And since this was a self-evident and undeniable fact, Johnny mulled over this revelation of a better self he never knew he possessed, he who was so unloveable that both parents had abandoned him. His aunt said this, in spite of the fact that the headmaster had sent one final warning to the effect that the boy was too disruptive. He was beginning to think that in spite of the incredible sums of money he charged for fees, these kinds of goings-on would give his precious school a bad name. He understood the boy's predicament, but surely a school yard could not be turned into a constant battleground!

"You think that *I am* a wonderful person?" Johnny asked to make sure that he had heard correctly. Wandia acted as if this conversation was perfectly normal in a person who had previously only communicated in angry grunts and growls.

"Of course Johnny, don't *you* think so?" Johnny thought about it and decided that even though he had not thought so before, he would think so in future.

"And that I am a hard working person?" Truly he couldn't remember doing a stroke of work of any kind in his entire life. Except fighting, of course.

"The thing is, Johnny, that there are some days in everyone's life that are so tough that just getting up to face the day requires extraordinarily hard work."

"Yes!" The boy was surprised that she understood so well.

After two days, when he could at last see out of his

132

bashed up eyes, Johnny went back to school. He was a year behind in his work. At the end of the first month, the teacher reluctantly decided that not only had a great miracle taken place in the boy's personality and behaviour, he was actually well ahead of his current class-mates, so he was promoted to the second class. By the end of the year he was easily at the top of his class. He had a sharp and retentive mind. However, once in a while, especially during his adolescence, the dark undercurrents in his soul would rumble frighteningly close to the surface.

But looking into the eyes of the twenty-three-year-old Johnny, Wandia was certain that he could not remember just how bad it had really been. Forgetfulness was one of the more wonderful gifts of childhood. So, deciding to re-bury the demons of bygone times, she only said,

"Thank you Johnny." The sentiment was shared by her husband.

"You were saying your father invited you to—?" his uncle prodded gently.

"He invited me to go and visit him in Canada, and I think that it might be a good idea for me to go, though I want you to know that this will always be my home, and, as I said, you will always be first in my heart."

Wandia could not help laughing at that. She realised that Johnny, unsure of what the future held for him, was hanging on to the only safe harbour he knew.

"Listen, son, even if that statement were true, I doubt if it will hold true for long. It is only when you are young that you think that love is exclusive, that if you love one person, or a small group of people, it would be some sort of betrayal to love anyone else. Love is a multifaceted thing, only the expression and manner of loving differs. The more you love, the more you can love." And then she added tongue-in-cheek, "Besides I suspect that before too long, some pretty girl is going to come around and make you forget you ever loved anybody else, and that too is in order; it is as it should be." Johnny smiled doubtfully which made his uncle say, looking at Wandia,

"Your aunt is right, you know. But some things you can only experience for yourself. Nobody can teach you about them. In any case I think that your going to Canada would be an excellent idea. You are just at the beginning of your long recess, so you have three clear months ahead of you. But as you know, your Aunt and I haven't had a chance to get away for so long that I am embarrassed to remember just how long. We were thinking of taking two weeks off to go visit my brother Odongo back at the farm in Njoro—it's been a long time and your aunt and I need a break. We would greatly appreciate it if you and Alicia stayed on to watch the guys and make sure that Gandhi doesn't play ball from morning till midnight and watch television the rest of the time."

"Of course, uncle! You don't need to ask, it will

be a pleasure. Take a month off if you like."

"I would, but I doubt if your aunt would want to be away from home for so long, besides we want you off to Canada as soon as possible, I think you will enjoy it tremendously."

"I am not too sure about that really. You know dad has a wife and a daughter."

"Don't be cowardly Johnny, besides I am almost certain that it is because of her that John finally came. I am sure that you will like her."

Later they talked to John and found that now that his quest was approaching the end he was eager to go back to his family. His coming to Africa had revived his spirit. Its youthful nations and peoples and their wholesome and simple approach to life, despite all kinds of calamities, was invigorating. Best of all, to nest within the bossom of the African family was to know the source of the strength of the African, which daily gave him the courage to face the knife-edge struggle for existence.

"I fervently hope that whatever else disappears or is eroded by modernism, the African concept of family will remain," said John on the eve of his departure.

"But you realise that as in all other places the family here is fighting a rearguard action for it's survival. It appears so much easier to be, not merely nucleus, but entirely individualistic, to care for no-one except yourself and your comfort. More and more people are willing to sacrifice the sense of belonging, and moorless, swim through the sea of unencumbered freedom." It was Aoro who said that, suddenly remembering that as the oldest brother, it had traditionally been his duty to call his siblings together for a celebration of one sort or another. He had been remiss in fulfilling this duty over a number of years. He decided that he would soon have to rectify the oversight.

The truth was that he had wonderful brothers and sisters as did Wandia, people who were willing to chip in and help a fellow out at the slightest sign of trouble. Each of them, to say nothing of their spouses and children, had for example turned up to help out during Danny's funeral, trying in every way possible to lighten the emotional and physical burden of death. *And it takes a foreigner to come and remind me that the most valuable, the most vital thing we Africans possess is our families. Of course the family can be a disadvantage if some able-bodied members turn into bloodsuckers, but I can hardly accuse my siblings of that.* They were all a ferociously independent lot.

"However," said Wandia thoughtfully, as if reading Aoro's mind, "it can not for a moment be assumed that the African concept of the family has no major drawbacks. For example, the tribe as a concept of a larger family is something that will haunt Africa well into the third millennium. Many people believe that though you should be good to your family and by extension your tribe, other people of other tribes or races don't matter that much and are frequently to be looked down upon with contempt and even with hostility. Of course politicians don't hesitate to fan this tribal arrogance and ethnic fear into open conflict for their own highly questionable ends."

"But the ethnic factor is not peculiar to Africa. People the world over prefer their own," John interjected. "It is natural."

"Agreed," Wandia answered, "but preference of your own should not lead to hatred of others."

However, not wanting to stray too deeply into a heated political discussion, she changed the subject.

"So do you think you will come back to us someday?"

But John was non-committal.

"You never know, and this *is* a beautiful country. If it is at all possible I should like to bring my wife to visit. In any case I can never thank you enough for everything you have done for me and my children. Those words still sound very strange in my ears. I had decided that I had long forfeited my right to knowing them. Indeed I have no rights, all I have is a gift which can never be repaid, and that's thanks to you."

"Oh come on man," Aoro said embarrassed. "We did nothing more than anyone else could have done, besides she was my sister."

"I don't for a moment believe that just anyone could have done what you did, and pretty few could have done it so well."

Wandia who knew that gratitude was one of the

rarest of virtues, accepted the thanks graciously and disappearing into her study came back with a little wrapped parcel. She gave it to John.

"To remember us by," she said simply.

"What is it?" asked John, turning it in his large capable hands.

"It is an audio-cassette."

"A cassette?"

"Yes. It's by the old Kenyan master David Amunga. It contains a song by the name *I am Going Back to Kenya* that is rather corny but which rings with nostalgia. He played it almost half a century ago—in the nineteen-fifties." She did not add that she had had to score dozens of music stores before she could get exactly what she wanted—at risk to life and limb—in a quaint little place on River Road aptly named *Wazee Hukumbuka*—which meant *Old People Remember*, which was an euphemism for 'old favourites'.

John was amazed and moved at the same time.

"Nineteen-fifties!" he said for lack of anything more intelligent to say.

Wandia laughed.

"But I assure you his music, to say nothing of his wisdom, is ageless."

"Thanks. I am sure I will love it." *I am truly among friends and my heart, to say nothing of my blood, is irrevocably interlinked with this land.*

138

EIGHT

LAKE NAKURU

WANDIA AND AORO took their four wheeler Suzuki, usually set aside for trips to the countryside, especially in April when the heavens opened with abandon. Wandia in particular felt that she needed some breathing space, unbound by limits and perimeters and other peoples' needs.

Two weeks without having to worry about whether Gandhi had finally succeeded in breaking his neck, or Lisa's unreasonable attack of nerves before a test which would finally prove to be a walkover, or Mugo's unexpected withdrawal into himself. She had become very worried about him. She settled deeper into the car seat and allowed a blank to settle over her mind. Eventually she fell asleep.

Without realising it she had allowed herself to get completely exhausted and drained, not just physically but more importantly, in the mind, perhaps even within her very soul. Too much had been demanded of her, but she had not replenished—there had not been time. She needed to contemplate Kenya's world famous vistas—great expanses of savanna grasslands, the colour of old gold; and sculpted escarpments marking out the Great Rift Valley whose floor was dotted by little toy lakes around which masses of pink and white flamingoes frolicked. The Great Rift had been formed when the earth had still been young and temperamental, given to heaving fits and gut-wrenching seizures; full of explosive hope and creative power. But the world was now old and jaded and very tired, as she herself felt.

Where in all this struggle and strife lay meaning and wisdom? Where had the spirit of daring and undaunted optimism gone? Where was hope? Where indeed was she going? Was she happy with the destination and the path she had chosen to get there? Was she truly free or a self-deluded victim of a pre-concluded destiny or of an inexorable evolution? Was there any point in trying so hard? *Where was the anchor to hold on to as time swirled at one's feet, going its heedless way and carrying all, all, with it?* Wandia rested her head on the head-rest behind her and thought —*I must be very tired to think this way.*

More than many others, she was a self-realised woman—happy with what life had given her and what she had wrought and wrestled from life through sheer determination, and by always remaining open to both people and ideas. Yet in what lay happiness if not in the knowledge that she had not lived in vain, but had been creative with her body and her mind and that in a certain sense at least, personal immortality consisted precisely in this implanting of parts of herself and her mind into others? To be barren and unproductive, at least of ideas for the good, was to be in the grip of disintegration and inevitable dissolution. Perhaps in gazing at the works of the master craftsman and in slowing down her pace awhile, her ailing soul would lift a little, the malaise go away from her heart and her mind regain its customary fecundity.

And then there was Danny's death.

I never really mourned him properly, she thought, gazing at the place in her heart that Danny had occupied, *I was resigned to the inevitability of his death, but still it took me by surprise and there was no time to really mourn him. God himself makes mourning a must if one is to be comforted, be healed. Perhaps my greatest fault is my utter sense of self-sufficiency. I act as if nothing can shake me, I am always in control, always in charge.*

Aoro looked down at his dozing wife with a rare compassion. Compassion was a sentiment one hardly dared express towards Wandia, but she was worn out, this woman who had given meaning to his life. *Of all men, I'm the luckiest.*

"I love you," he said simply.

The farm in Njoro was now solely under the able management of Odongo Sigu, Aoro's youngest brother, a burly and powerful looking man. He was assisted by his wife Jael, a friendly and gregarious person—who nevertheless managed her husband and five children with impressive efficiency. Opiyo, Odongo's twin brother, had sold his share of the farm to his brother, preferring to live in Nakuru Town with his wife— a well dressed and highly made-up woman who had been truly horrified at the idea that anyone at all, least of all her husband, should expect her to touch soil except as a ceremonial gesture during funerals.

Jael was normally up at five, woke her husband and children by five-thirty and all were ready for breakfast by six. By six-thirty her husband made his way to the dairy to supervise the milking while the older children started on their way to school, about a kilometre and a half away. At seven-thirty she walked the fourth child, four-year-old Aoro, to his nursery school about a kilometre away at the church hall. On the way she told stories and sang songs to whichever child was lucky enough to be in nursery school at any particular time. This was the way they would remember their mother all their lives, not the not-so-rare times she had used her slippers to swat recalcitrant bottoms.

Jael was a remarkable woman. This year alone they had twenty acres under wheat, ten under maize, five under potatoes and two acres under an assortment of horticultural crops supposedly for home use, but each year she seemed to have an impressive surplus for the market at Nakuru. She spent quite a bit of time behind the wheel of her little pick-up delivering farm produce.

Aoro had been touched when his brother had named his second and youngest son after him.

"Oh, but he will be a doctor one day, just like his uncle," Jael had said happily. Everyone had smiled indulgently for had not her husband Odongo been the dunce of the Sigu family and had she herself not dropped out of high school—due to lack of fees, yes, but a drop-out was a drop-out. But a few years later the smiles had changed to whistles of amazement and chagrin when her oldest child, Elizabeth had passed her primary exam at the top of the entire district, was the third best in the province and probably among the top twenty in the entire country. With that the young lady had also won a scholarship to the top national school for girls.

"*Hala*! But her father never could negotiate his way beyond 10 + 10!" someone remarked.

"That has not prevented him from being a highly successful farmer and I believe richer than all of us put together. Don't be deceived by the simplicity of his personal life-style."

"She is a throwback!" some other family member remarked, his pride wounded. He meant a throwback to some illustrious ancestor on the father's side.

"Nonsense. Her mother, behind all those smiles, is one smart woman! Besides she has a way with her husband and children."

Jael busied herself with her guests, wanting them to have the best that she could offer.

"But you don't have to wake up early at all. I know just how hard doctors work and how tired you must be," she said solicitously. *What a nice person,* Wandia thought, relaxing immediately in her sister-in-law's presence. *She will succeed where others fail because she does not dwell on what can't be done, but rather on what can be done—and does it.*

Every afternoon they drove to Lake Nakuru—a bird watchers' paradise, if ever there was one, with over 400 species—warbling, waddling and wading, in and around the lake.

"I have always loved the flamingoes—Nakuru was my boyhood town, and one never really outgrows such things. My dad used to take us for picnics by the lake once in a while and we loved it, though I fear we were rather boisterous boys. Sometimes I think Gandhi was sent to make me pay for my boyhood escapades—though I was not as impervious to knowledge as that guy seems to be."

Wandia was surprised to discover that there were a lot of animals too, including the inimitable warthog, which, in this haven, strutted about as if he was sole lord of all he saw. At least in other game parks, a warthog had to watch out for lions, leopards and hyenas to say nothing of wild dogs, all of whom dearly loved fresh warthog for breakfast. But here at Lake Nakuru, such nightmares were so far away or so rare as to be nothing more than an unpleasant dream which occasionally came true. A warthog could live out its days in peace, to see its children and its children's children unto the third generation.

There were several types of antelopes including lots of waterbuck and reedbuck, some bushbuck and many Impala. However, neither of the two was that knowledgeable about the subject and as there was no guide to arbitrate, there were almost constant arguments as to whether an antelope was an Impala or a Grant's Gazelle or something else, but of course both at least knew what a Thomson's Gazelle looked like and thus whenever a rufous-coloured Gazelle with a black stripe across its abdomen went past, both nodded sagely and declared in unison;

"It's a Tommy!" Which of course was the most basic piece of information in a Kenyan park.

But it was the birds that were the attraction of Lake Nakuru. At least several hundred thousand Lesser and Greater Flamingo were massed along the western shores of the lake, not, of course, that either Aoro or Wandia could tell the difference between the two species anyway. The birds were making a terrific racket! Every once in a while a group of them would take to the air in perfect choreography, legs stretched out straight behind them like dancers, pinkish wings flapping in unison. They would land at some other point with equal dexterity and grace, with the merest skid on the surface of the water before coming to a complete stop.

"Oh how perfect!" Wandia cried. She was a person

very much susceptible to beauty and one can hardly improve on the Flamingo for sheer elegance, grace and beauty.

"It's like a whole bunch of models out for their summer holidays," remarked Aoro. Wandia laughed at the comparison.

There were tall gawky Herons, and self-opinionated pelicans —very full of their own importance; there were comorants and storks, ibises, ducks and geese, and many others.

They took turns at the binoculars and at reading the descriptions in their bird-watching book; and their delight at successfully identifying a bird was so inordinate and disproportionate to the actual usefulness of the exercise that Aoro remarked.

"It is an instinct of the human race to want to name things. No wonder God brought the animals in Eden to be named by Adam. I think I understand exactly how he felt when God brought him a Flamingo or a Pelican to name."

Wandia laughed and she realised, with renewed wonder, what a great thing it was to be alive—senses tingling, mind expansive—taking in everything. She felt restored—not just refreshed, as if her life had slowly been ebbing away, but now was surging back at a high tide.

Finally the two weeks were over and it was time to go home. They spent the last morning of their stay with Jael and Odongo and the children. Jael had cooked as if this was to be everyone's last meal on earth.

"I'm so happy you decided to come and visit us ,"
Odongo kept repeating until Aoro was consumed with
guilt for having neglected his brother so. It was clear
that he and Jael looked up to Wandia and himself with
something akin to hero-worship.

"You must come and stay with us soon—come on
my Mark's birthday," Aoro told him. "Bring the kids.
We'll all get together and have a great time."

"That would be wonderful. It's been a long time."

Wandia decided to go for a walk with the
clamouring children, to take them off Jael's hands for
a little while.

"Auntie, we can show you our little house deep in
the forest," said Oloo conspiratorially and his sister
Maria nodded vigorously. So Auntie carried young
Aoro piggy-back and off they went to look for the house
deep in the forest. The path was well trodden. Wandia
loved footpaths. They reminded her of the hilly
countryside of her youth. A foot-path disappearing up
a hill or round a corner—suggested to her the passionate
connection between man and earth, an intimacy paved
by human feet searching for the living heart of the
world—for the destiny of humankind and the world in
which they live are intimately and inextricably
intertwined. *For we are born to the world, live in it all
our days and one day it will enfold us lovingly back to
itself once again. No wonder some tribes call her
Mother Earth.*

Little Aoro was having a great time. He was a big,

chunky boy and it was a long time since anyone had carried him piggy-back. Once, on his way to school he had asked his mother to carry him— just for the fun of it.

"No way!" had been the brief reply. "You will dislocate my spine." But today was his lucky day. Auntie Wandia went up dizzyingly in his heartfelt opinion. If asked, he would have put her in heaven alongside the saints whom he had been told were very wonderful people.

Deep in the forest turned out to be a clump of trees about one hundred meters from the house.

Shrubs and lianas growing at the foot of two trees had formed a canopy under which a child could hide and nurse its angers and disappointments, its hopes and aspirations. And Wandia thought with some wonder: *all of us need to get away sometimes—even the little children!*

She realised that this hide-out had never been shown to any adult and it was high honour for her to be brought here. So she got down on her hands and knees and crawled into the 'house.' She lay down on her back and the children crawled in around her. After some minutes of quiet and personal meditation, during which Wandia tried to imagine what a child thought about and the children in their turn tried to imagine what an adult thought about, if he thought at all, Maria piped up and said the most natural thing in the world,

"Tell us a story Auntie!"

And why not, thought Wandia, *of what use is an aunt if she can't tell a story?*

"Once upon a time there lived a little boy called Osin who could not smile..." Wandia fell into and spent an hour telling stories invented on the spur of the moment.

Oloo and Maria were enthralled and kept urging her to tell more, but little Aoro was soon fast asleep. When they woke him up he yawned and announced, in tones that made it sound as if he had not seen food for several days:

"I am hungry!"

So they all went back up the path to the old farmhouse that had been built by old Mark and Elizabeth Sigu. Little had changed. Wandia left the children and went to the little graveyard at the back of the house to pay homage to the dead. There was old Mark Sigu and his wife Elizabeth resting peacefully side by side. And there was Becky, her life and death emanating utter sadness even after all these years. There was a little girl called Anette who had been twin sister to Odongo Sigu's eldest daughter Elizabeth, but who had died soon after birth, much to her mother's sorrow—the only wound in that good woman's heart. And more recently Danny, her own baby, who had been brought here to rest with his kith and kin.

She sat with Danny for a long time and then getting up released him from her heart. *Go baby go. Go and be free and happy and well!*

149

They had a feast of a lunch outside at the back veranda. It was a rather congenial day for April. At around four o'clock Aoro and Wandia finally took their leave and started the journey back to the city. Knowing that she would be cooped up in the city for God alone knew how long again, Wandia drank in the scenery as they left the lake-dotted floor of the Rift Valley (which in the two hour stretch between Nakuru and Nairobi boasted not less than three lakes—Nakuru, Elementaita and Naivasha).

It was quite late by the time they reached the lakeside town of Naivasha. The brilliant blue evening sun made picturesque and mystical-looking shapes in the western sky. Wandia noted one that looked like an open-mouthed crocodile with a crown of molten silver around its head. At one point a little black tower-shaped cloud detached itself and went to rest right at the heart of the sun, blue light streaming around it making it look like something left over after a science fiction catastrophe. *Nature is inimitable in its beauty and power and endless variety*, she thought to herself, strangely moved by the spectacle.

Too soon they approached Nairobi with all its hustle and bustle. As Aoro pulled up to the house, the children tumbled out of the house yelling happily. Amidst hugs and kisses Wandia noticed that Gandhi was missing.

"Where's Gandhi?" she asked in alarm. Everyone turned around and as if on cue Gandhi walked out of the door holding up a poster emblazoned:

WELCOME TO THE ZOO!

in his best handwriting.

They hugged the little tyke in relief.

"For a moment there I thought the police had finally decided to come for you," his mother said.

Gandhi looked belligerently at Anwarite.

"Have you been telling on me already?"

"No, but I will soon. It will require several days. I have carefully listed everything you have done from the time mummy went away." Gandhi dived at his mincing sister.

"Children! Children!"

And Wandia knew that the holiday was over, but it was good to be surrounded by the children again—angels, felons and all.

Ten

SYBIL

JOHN SHIVERED A LITTLE as he left the warmth of the air conditioned airport lounge. His body remembered with longing the brilliant sunshine in Nairobi, but then, life was an inexorable onward march. He saw Sybil and Andrea waving at him from among the waiting throng and he headed his luggage trolley towards them. The two made a concerted rush towards him and he gave them both a mighty bear hug. Andrea, walking backwards in her excitement at having her daddy back, started talking about several things all at once, but Sybil, her hand in his, searched his face for clues of what might have transpired during his trip to Africa.

She had very dark almost black hair, with a heart shaped face and fine brown rather slow moving eyes that rested long on things and moved only reluctantly. When spoken to, she had a trick of turning her head towards the speaker while her eyes remained gazing at whatever had their attention only to trail slowly in the direction of new interest. It was disconcerting, but once you had her attention it was also total.

"Daddy what was it like in Africa? Did you see any lions?"

"Er, no." Andrea looked at him in disappointed disbelief. She was a very high-spirited child, with her mother's face and colouring. But while Sybil was a small compact person, very petite, Andrea was tall and gangly like her father, and at ten was almost as tall as her mother. She was already showing definite artistic powers —a third generation artist on her mother's side, but then again she had been surrounded with brilliant colour from her earliest infancy and her nursery had been a technicolor dreamhouse where pink elephants stared in disbelief at blue giraffes.

Her grandfather, Andrew Stanley, after whom she had been named, had been a notable artist in his time, but had died in a car crash, before full self-realisation. He had been merely forty-three, but a prolific man both artistically and otherwise—leaving a widow and five children aged fourteen and below. Sybil, the oldest, was her father's dearest buddy and he had affectionately called her Billie.

The shock had lasted for about a year for Billie. It would have lasted longer had she not realised that her mother had simply fallen apart and was showing no signs of recovery. As a result, her brothers, Douglas and Brett aged twelve and eight respectively, were spending more time in the streets than in the classroom, though they turned up faithfully for whatever meals could be had. The twins, April and Dolores, almost six, were looking lost and unattended. The meals, which had formerly been prepared with loving care, were sketchy, to say the least.

Someone had to take over. Billie looked around for this someone and realised that if she didn't do it no one would.

Even at that age, Sybil was a single-minded kind of person. She called in her brothers and after painting a gory picture of the kind of things that were likely to happen to boys who did not go to school (which left the two little rascals unmoved), she informed them that from then on anyone who did not attend classes and was not seen to actually do so would not be allowed to eat.

"Yeah?" said Douglas, looking most unimpressed. For the last one year, meals had consisted of grabbing whatever you could out of the fridge and wolfing it down practically where you were standing. Sometimes their mother forgot to shop and the two boys somehow managed to convince her to give them money for hamburgers and hot dogs from the fast food place a couple of blocks away. Guilt ridden and depressed she would comply.

Billie realised that several things had to be done before her authority could be felt in that household. First she had a talk with her mother.

"Mum, do you know that the boys are going wild and hardly go to school any more?"

She hadn't known. The revelation made her shrink into herself even more and this made Billie sorry for her, but she promised herself that she would never love a man so much if all it did to you was leave you completely incapacitated. Indeed before she met John, who looked lost and bewildered, she had had no sustained interest in men at all. But John was older and in a vague way reminded her of her late father, a man who could be affectionate without demanding a pound of flesh and a gallon of blood in payment.

"It's okay mum, just leave it to me. But don't give the boys any more money. Once a week you will take me to do proper shopping and then I will do the cooking." Billie knew that money was not a serious problem because her father had had a hefty insurance cover and her mother had a little money of her own from some property her parents had owned.

"You know how to cook?" her mother asked in surprise. Billie hadn't the foggiest idea but she said bravely,

"What I don't know I will soon learn."

"Okay." It was an easy way out, but Billie thinking ahead added,

"By the way they are looking for a librarian to run the downtown library. It would keep you busy and also bring in some money. Dad did want us all to have a good education, you know, and I am sure you loved him too much to let that dream go up in smoke, didn't you?" she asked pointedly, though her face was all wide-eyed innocence. Her mother blinked her eyes in dismay at this demand upon her time and person, but the young lady stood her ground.

"Okay, I'll look into it." But her daughter, knowing she had no intention of leaving the house to face the world again, bided her time. She knew that her mother was a qualified librarian even though she had not worked at it for a long time. Besides, the insurance money could not last forever. When she got an opportunity, she rummaged through her mother's drawers for the certificates and references she had seen there a long time back in better days. At the earliest opportunity, she took them to the chief librarian who knew her because she had regularly haunted the place practically from the time she could read.

"Hi, Mr. Grant."

"Hi, Sybil. I don't see too much of you these days, is everything okay at home?"

"Pretty much okay, Mr. Grant, but I told my mother about that job you are advertising and she is very keen—though she has been unwell lately, she misses dad a lot you know."

"I am sorry to hear that, I hope it is not too serious."

"No, she's getting better every day. She gave me her papers to bring to you." She slid them over. Mr. Grant looked at them.

"But these are very good. Even though she hasn't worked for a long time I am sure we could use her."

"Oh I'm sure she can brush up pretty fast, she is very bright you know." *Just spineless*, she added to herself with unchildlike cynicism. "Why don't you give her a call?"

"I'll do that." He knew Mrs Stanley from a distance. In spite of all those children she was a good looking woman in her late thirties. He was fifty and still a bachelor. There must have been some good reasons why he had remained so for so many years, only problem was that he couldn't quite remember what they were. Sybil headed for the section on Domestic Science, and began to study cookery as seriously as if she was studying for an exam. After several mishaps and one or two near catastrophes whose only results were blackened oxides of various items which had previously been human food, she eventually became an excellent cook and finally took over that aspect of family life.

She was slightly disappointed, but not surprised when her mother married Robert Grant barely two years after Andrew Stanley's death—she understood very well that her mother was the kind of woman who simply had to have a man around, and the boys did need a man's firm hand, though she was often surprised at how often this man's hand turned out to be her own slim but tough one. The two love birds were too preoccupied to be bothered with the nitty-gritties of raising a couple of teenage boys. And after the practice with her brothers, the twins, April and Dolores simply had no choice but to follow the straight and narrow as prescribed by one Sybil Stanley. However, by the time she was through with them all, she simply had had enough of the whole business of children and of raising them.

It was the librarian's job which saved Anne Stanley's sanity and her family, to say nothing of getting her a much needed companion. In his own way Robert Grant was a good, if easy-going man. He had been a bachelor for so long that one could really not expect too much of him.

Sybil, true to her word, started to use food as a weapon. Her brothers, after being starved several times, decided that going back to school was the less painful alternative. They eventually turned out into very fine men, a fact in which Sybil took a great deal of pride.

"By the time I was fifteen, I was as busy as the old woman in a shoe and her many children. I have decided that that experience was enough for me. I hope you don't feel that we have to have children," she had told John when she agreed to marry him.

"Not particularly," John answered not entirely honestly. He didn't tell her that somewhere in Africa he had children. It was then still too painful to want to discuss. They were therefore quite surprised when three years after their marriage, Andrea made her turbulent entry into the world despite an all-out effort in pregnancy prevention on her mother's part.

Andrea's insistent questioning of her father about lions brought her back to the present.

"You didn't see any, not even one?"

"No," John answered feeling both defensive and sorry that he had forgotten that he had been duty-bound to see as much as possible for Andrea's sake. But there had been other things more important than lions on his mind. Andrea looked at him as if she would have liked to court-martial him for such negligence.

"But I thought they were everywhere!" she exclaimed not willing to accept that one could go all the way to Africa and not see such a basic thing as a lion, to say nothing of elephants, buffaloes and leopards.

"Actually they are not that easy to see, that is unless you want to see a caged lion. You have to expend quite a bit of energy to see a lion and many other wild animals as well."

"That's enough about lions now. Your father's had a very long journey and is very tired."

"Oh mum!" protested Andrea who wanted to be told everything at once.

"Yes miss!"

The trio finally reached the car and got in. Sybil was a competent driver and John allowed himself to relax and even doze a little. He *was* very tired.

After a shower and something to eat he felt more equal to answering at least the more insistent of his daughter's questions before lying down to sleep off the jet lag.

When he woke up it was four in the morning and he had slept for fifteen hours. He turned and saw Sybil sitting by the window looking out into the night. This in itself was not anything new, she often did that, sitting absolutely still and immobile, looking intently at the shapes in the night. But immediately he was fully awake, John realised that she was looking intently, not out the window, but at him. He got out of bed and padded to her side.

"So what happened?" she asked without preamble.

"It was not as bad as I feared, but the boy was very difficult."

She smiled enigmatically in the half-light;

"Boys always are." She was thinking of the adventures of Brett and Douglas, in what seemed like a life-time ago.

"I guess you are more of an expert in that area than I am," John said, laughing. He liked his brothers-in-law. Douglas was a tall powerful, but very friendly man. He was vice-president of a large construction company and was married with two children. Brett Stanley, thirty-two, was a professor of linguistics at the University of Toronto. He was a very cultured and widely travelled man in whose erudite presence one was liable to feel rather uneducated. As if that was not enough, he spoke several foreign languages fluently.

John had been an only child of elderly parents, now long dead—he was after all in his mid-fifties—and he appreciated the family reunions that the five noisy Stanley siblings could organise. April had married young and had three children. Dolores was a high-powered career bureaucrat and at thirty did not seem to have room in her life for husband and children.

"I am very interested in the girl, what was she like?" Sybil asked.

"She is an absolutely lovely person, very gifted, but also very delicate, almost fragile. I suppose her start in life was a bit tough—part fault of mine, I agree."

"So what does she do?"

"She teaches music and I mean the real thing," he could not help unbidden paternal pride from creeping into his voice. "She is also taking a Master's Degree in the same."

"My, my! How did a thorough-going philistine like you surround yourself with all these artistic souls?" He heard more than saw the gentle laughter in her voice.

"I don't really know, but I suppose there is something attractive in my caveman personality," he joked. "Something that makes evanescent artistic types feel safe and protected."

"I'm not evanescent!" And he had to concur. She was just about the toughest little person he knew.

"Well, you are atypical."

"All artists are atypical— it's almost a trademark. They simply regard most things from a different or unusual angle. Tell me more about the girl."

He wondered at her interest.

"She is very beautiful..."

"Like her mother?"

He paused, afraid of where this might lead. Women

were strange, you never knew what they might spring on you when you least expected it. They seemed to enjoy a man's chagrin. After all he was a man who had been very much in love with two different, very different, women. And he had loved them. He was too honest and simple a person to pretend even to himself that he had not loved Becky even after all these years. But love was a many-faced thing; who could pin it down like a butterfly and say—*this is it?*

"Yes and no," he finally ventured. She turned her face away and smiled in the darkness enjoying his sudden cageyness. She could almost hear him think.

"And what do you mean by that?"

"I mean that her mother was exotically and flawlessly beautiful. Alicia is not in the same league, but then I never did meet anyone who was. The girl has an inner radiance which is still fighting to come through. Her mother had an external sheen, you could look at it for hours without feeling that you had plumbed the person—she was a secret never to be understood, perhaps even by herself. Both had, have a childlike quality—but in the mother it was brittle and carelessly cruel, as many children can be; in the daughter it is loveable and human, which shows that maturity has occurred, but has not hardened into cynicism. I fear for her, that someone might terribly wound her, and in her case there will be no question of surviving."

Sybil remained thoughtfully silent. The girl sounded like a female version of her father.

"I know that you have not asked and that in reality it does not matter; she has been dead these many years and believe me when I say she no longer has a pull on me. But I did love her, very much—I'm afraid I am that kind of a man—I never did perfect a hit and run personality. I love to stay with those I love. But I could characterise my love for her as intense, and almost consuming. Now I am old enough to recognise that there is always something self-seeking in loving anyone like that for it means that essentially you are in love with a dream and you don't want to wake up and face reality—you would much rather have the deception of the dream. Is this perhaps the reason she turned so violently against me? Was I perhaps the only person who could have saved her, by first knowing her and then helping her escape from herself? Was this the root of her self- destructive anger which almost destroyed us all? I guess I never will know and for her it's too late.

But as for you, my love, I love you more every day, and the more I know you the more I love you. I must live a long life in order to know you more and more so that at the end of my life I can say that truly you are my other self, my very self—only better than my mere self."

***

HE HAD BEEN STANDING just behind her chair and he put out his hand to touch her face. It was wet with tears. He had been like a wounded animal and she had generously and selflessly nursed him back to health without really being sure of where his true loyalties lay.

"What I am trying to say is not that I've never loved anybody else, but you I love with my being, with my life—which you have given back to me; and to love a woman like you is to be alive, which is what I am and want to be, so that in loving you I may finally realise who I am and why I am here."

"Thanks," was all she could come up with. She felt humbled, which was a rare and extraordinary thing. She carefully wrapped it up and put it away to be examined later as one would examine a hitherto undescribed species, unknown to humankind—she, Sybil Stanley, humbled by something a man had to say!

"Tell me about little Johnny," she finally managed to say, her voice sounding strange even in her own ears.

"Little Johnny, my leg! He is a tall man who will soon graduate from medical school. But that boy is something else, he gave me a hard time of it, I can tell you that. He was terribly traumatised by the whole business of the divorce and in his mind I was naturally the villain. It took a great deal of persuasion to get him to give me at least a fair trial. It came as a surprise to him to hear that in spite of whatever pet theories he had about me, it was his mother who divorced me not the other way round. Somehow everyone assumed that since I had reason, I was the one who started the proceedings. Anyway the long and short of it is that both will be here come October." He went round and stood directly in front of her and gathering courage from the darkness continued, "You know something, I was thinking while out there in Africa that it would be a wonderful thing if you and I had another child."

She gaped at him. The morning light was beginning to filter in and she could see the outline of his face and his mad smile.

"What!"

He must have had too much of the African sun.

"Well, I was staying with this wonderful African couple and guess how many children they have."

"That's Africa and this is Canada, for heaven's sake! Things are different here. Besides I'm simply too busy to consider that kind of madness."

"I know, darling, but so are they. Believe it or not she is a Professor of Haematology and chairperson of an entire medical department in a teaching hospital. And she has six children to say nothing of my two and one other child belonging to a deceased brother."

"Jesus!"

"No, I am not saying that you have to have six children, but one more couldn't hurt surely?" He realised too late that that was the worst choice of words even a fool like him could come up with.

"Of course it would hurt like the bloodiest hell, but what would you know about that anyway? If you did, we would not be having this strange conversation! Besides, if she is really a doctor she should know better."

"She does," he said quietly, remembering Wandia's serene face and lovely children. Something in his voice caught her attention, some echo of a deep-seated longing. "But listen, darling, that was an offhand suggestion, perhaps not a very opportune one, I can see that. Forget it. I love you too much to make you do anything you don't want to do." But she, sitting absolutely still, had stopped listening to his words. She was straining to hear those echoes in his voice —echoes from a 'dark' continent.

It was also beginning to dawn on her just how much she loved this man. *But another child!* She was almost thirty-eight, wasn't that the age when you were supposed to be more likely to get a baby with Down Syndrome? Feeling uncharacteristically uncertain she tentatively voiced this fear which she thought would appeal to science and therefore to reason.

"Am I not at an age where the possibility of having a child with Down Syndrome is very likely?"

"I suppose so. These people also had a child with Down Syndrome." His voice was carefully non-committal. It really wasn't because of the Sigus that he wanted Sybil and himself to have another child, it was something entirely to do with themselves and his renewed sense of the wonder of being.

He didn't fully understand it himself, but he was beginning to think that the death of Western culture would not be from external foes but from internal inanition whose surest sign was the unwillingness of large numbers of people to have any thing more than the token child or none at all. Surely what good could be better than a human child?

Then he realised that that kind of thinking would get one hanged by a whole crowd of self-proclaimed modern-day doomsday prophets. The human child was at par with any baby animal and was of less importance than the panda and the white rhino and a host of other animals thought to be endangered. *It was a good thing the dinosaurs passed out of existence so long ago, otherwise they too would no doubt have been on that list. Are we servants and stewards of the earth and its treasures or are we its slaves?* And he marvelled how drastically his thinking had changed.

"Down Syndrome! How old is she?" Sybil asked in shock.

"Actually it was their eldest son so she must have been in her twenties. Their youngest son, who must have been born after she turned forty, is a very bright and charming little person by the name of Mark. If he has any problem at all it's probably too much brains. The son with Down Syndrome died a couple of months back from bone cancer."

"Jesus!" she repeated, not that she was a person given to swearing, but what else could a sane person say when faced by someone who was having an attack of momentary insanity?

"They all seemed to have loved him very much, he must have been quite a character. These are generous people with big hearts."

"And by that I suppose you mean that I'm not."

"As far as I am concerned, you are in a class of your own. You are the most generous person I have ever met, it's just that we are looking at this from two different angles. And God knows I owe you my life, my sanity, my happiness. I have no right to ask for anything more. It was a thought, that's all. Please forget it."

And that precisely was what she could not do.

She wandered away to her studio where no one was permitted to enter except by invitation. She stood in front of her latest completed work and watched the newborn light playing tenderly on it. It was an arrangement of T-shaped wires whose shadows threw shades of different shapes on the background. The shapes, now rhomboidal and angular, now wavy and mobile, varied according to the angle of the light and the movement of the eyes. It was only on moving near that one realised that it was not a painting. She was also an accomplished painter and especially liked to do children at play.

There was one such uncompleted painting of a waif-like little girl sitting on her heels and intently studying something whose nature had yet to become clear. She had on a tiny yellow tunic that only came down to mid thigh, her little hands on each side of her childishly innocent knees. On her face was the inscrutability of a child's mind. She could have been three or four or perhaps a little older, but small for her age. Sybil's eyes rested for a while on this child of her imagination.

She believed that the true nature of her talent lay in the fact that somewhere along the line she had recognised that she was merely a conduit for a greater creative force. All she ever did was to remove obstacles from its way and place herself in a position of willingness to be led—sometimes slowly, sometimes with bursts of creative insight and power, but always following to see where a piece of work might lead. At the beginning of the work she had a concept, yes, but more often than not the concept took off on its own and the difference between a mediocre piece of work and an excellent one often depended on whether she had had the courage to follow where the concept led.

It was the modern art that sold widely and well, but she did the painting simply to renew her soul—each one was highly detailed and was tenderly executed. Whenever someone bought one of these, she scrutinised them as closely as one does when placing a baby for adoption. Were the prospective owners people who would love and cherish the child of her creativity? But even if they were, there was always a wrench when a painting had been bought. It was truly like losing a most beloved child, upon which one had travailed and laboured.

Sybil drifted to the painting of the child again. She stood looking at it for a long time and then, with tears in her eyes, she grabbed a brush and started to work with a frenzied urgency —to exorcise the maternal instinct with a brilliance that she would only rarely equal again in her lifetime. That painting, pulsating with the mystery of childhood—was destined to win countless awards, and copies of it to hang on countless walls.

When she failed to emerge five hours later, John, who had already made breakfast, taken Andrea to school, come back and sat around for a couple of hours, decided to take his courage in his hands and approach the lioness in her lair.

Cup of coffee in one hand, he knocked gently on the door. There was no answer. He knocked again and when the silence continued his fear started to mount. *It would serve you right if she left you, you idiot. What does it matter anyway? You have more than your fair share of everything. A child will not make that much difference to this relationship.* But in his heart he knew, he just knew, it would. It would enrich both of them in ways they did not even suspect. And Andrea would be in seventh heaven. At one stage she had shed tears when mummy had said a definitive and final no—a little dog was possible, but a brother? Never. Andrea had eventually resigned herself to the powers that be.

John finally pushed his way into the room. He found her curled up in a fetal position fast asleep on a rug. The poor thing had probably been up half the night—she had always been something of a night-owl. He put the cup down and gently lifted her up in his arms. As he straightened he saw the breath-taking painting that would come to be known as *The Waif in Yellow*. It had captured the nostalgia of the lost simplicity of childhood—the capacity to wonder and be totally absorbed in little nameless things. This was art that would speak to generations upon generations. He did not know too much about it, but surely this must be what a masterpiece looked like? And it wasn't even complete yet!

He walked along the corridors of the large house until he reached the spacious bedroom which reflected Sybil's tastes and personality more than any other room in the house, apart from her studio.

"The place to work and the place to rest, away from prying eyes—these are important," she once said.

Gently he placed her on the bed, lifted the covers and rolled her under. He made her head comfortable and then went to sit in the chair she had sat on during their conversation last night. It looked out into the dying garden, and made him think of that other garden thousands of miles away. Yet only three days ago he had been there dozing in the bright sun and gazing at its lush tropical plants.

Once again he thought of the unusual turns his life had taken. On the balance perhaps he had made more mistakes than most men, but he had been lucky. He was thankful that he had never been vengeful or even consumed by hatred. He had tried according to his lights not to cause anyone unnecessary hurt, at least not actively. That he had hurt his own children due to too great a tendency to passivity was his one great sorrow. To the children that he had and to others if they ever came, he would try to be the best possible father—from the lessons of over half a century.

He would soon be fifty-five and yet he felt like he was twenty-five, and just starting out, only this time he had the benefit of the experience of a lifetime. One thing he would never get another chance to be, was a better son. His parents had been old and he had been young and eager to get on with his life. He had loved them, yes, but simply never had time for them. Yet he had been a most beloved son, conceived long after his parents had despaired of having a child. His mother had died uttering excuses on his behalf. He really had a lot to make up for. As did most of his generation. To them a lot had been given, and they had taken and taken yet again. Little had been demanded of them except that they strive to be happy.

But in what lay happiness? Surely the abundance of physical and spiritual well being, with little material pain should have guaranteed happiness? Yet many of his contemporaries were terribly unhappy, several times divorced, satiated and jaded, appetites dulled with untrammelled and cheap sex and too much of everything.

Yet, thought John, *I am lucky because I know that at this moment and in these days, I have tasted happiness. I have had the good luck to recognise my mistakes and the chance to rectify those that can be rectified and to move ahead. I have had the chance to touch other people's lives positively and to be gentle*

*with my own self too. Not many are this lucky. People
flail themselves mercilessly or indulge themselves
uncontrollably.*

*I freely chose to love this woman. I will love her
with my body and my mind, not just because she is
loveable and deserves to be loved, which is true enough,
but may not always be the case. But I recognise that I
need to love, because in loving precisely this woman
will I recreate and find myself and the purpose for which
I am here.*

173

ELEVEN

BRETT

SYBIL, JOHN AND ANDREA met Alicia and Johnny at the Airport. Alicia looked calm but remote while Johnny looked uncertain of his welcome. *What a good looking pair!* Sybil thought, taking in Alicia's olive heart-shaped face and well-proportioned body and Johnny's athletic grace. Sybil, not one given to standing on ceremony, went first to Alicia and then to Johnny and in turn gave each a hug. It was a cold blustery day and she said with a wide wave of her left arm,

"It is not the most welcoming day to arrive in Canada, but I can assure you that I am so glad you have finally arrived that my heart must surely warm up the weather a bit. Unfortunately the days are not really going to improve at all, if any thing they will get worse, but I am sure we will have a thousand things to do together."

"Mummy, you forgot to introduce me!" bleated Andrea from behind her parents.

"Oh and this is Andrea, our little girl."

"I'm not so little—I will soon be eleven." To prove it she stretched out her hand in a most grown up fashion. Her step-brother and sister shook it solemnly and both liked her immediately in spite of the mischief lurking somewhere in her eyes. They instantly recognised a kindred spirit to Gandhi who was probably up to no good at this very moment back home in Kenya. This made them feel instinctively welcome and at home.

"You remind me of my cousin—he is just about your age," Alicia remarked her eyes resting on Andrea.

"Is he an interesting person?"

"I can assure you that nothing boring ever happens around Gandhi; he leads a busy life."

"Oh, that's an interesting name. Is he named after that great man in India?"

"That very one."

"I think I would like to meet Gandhi," Andrea said thoughtfully.

"Oh he is long, long, dead," John supplied.

"The Indian one yes, but the one I want to meet is alive, isn't he?" Everyone laughed and whatever tension there was, dissolved.

Alicia liked Canada immediately. In the Brampton suburb in which they lived, the houses were largely constructed of timber, which she found delightful. Also they had nothing more than a picket fence or nothing at all, which was a relie after the claustrophobic perimeter walls surrounding almost all houses in Nairobi out of fear of burglary, theft, and often enough, armed robbery. She remembered the hordes of unemployed youth who loitered around the city. The crime rate was in such high proportions that some wag had decided to give Nairobi a new name–Nairobbery.

"Things can be just as bad here in some ways," Sybil told her. "But I suppose people value their freedom more than they fear burglars."

Sybil went out of her way to make Alicia feel wanted and welcome. They shopped, visited galleries, museums and whatever else looked interesting. The whole family spent an afternoon at Niagara and Johnny and Alicia could not get over the sheer size and beauty of the falls.

"Most of it belongs to us," bragged Andrea. "The Americans only have that tiny little bit over there."

"That's the US?" Alicia queried.

"Yes, the border's right over there." She pointed again. There was a cold mist thrown up by the impact of the falling waters. Johnny shivered a little. The place was rather overwhelming and even primeval. It reminded one just how puny man was.

There was a boat with yellow jacketed people in it going up and down the horse shoe-shaped lake at the bottom of the falls.

"What the heck are those people doing in there?" Johnny asked Sybil.

"Oh, they are just having fun."

"Fun!" Alicia was amazed at what some people called fun. "I thought for a moment that they were life savers."

"But people have died here in terrible accidents," supplied Andrea in her ghostliest voice, her brown eyes dancing with wicked delight, hectic colour surging up and down her cheeks. Her mother made as if to grab her but she skilfully evaded the outstretched arm.

"It's true! It's true."

"I know it's true, but do you have to take such wicked delight in it?" Andrea tried to look dutifully sad but failed miserably.

"What's that?" Johnny asked pointing at a tower to one side.

"That's an observation tower, would you like to go up and get a bird's eye-view of things?" John asked.

"Yes of course!"

"Would you girls be interested in coming with us?" John asked the rest.

"No thank-you!" they said in unison, shaking their heads as if such madness was unthinkable. After all they were three highly intelligent women, why would they want to go up for a dose of vertigo? There were more interesting things to do during man's short sojourn on this earth. Such as shop.

John's heart was brimming with the thought that at last, *at last!* he had all his children with him. He was not a particularly religious person, but he felt like praying and giving thanks for the miracle of reunion,

177

of family. He breathed in deeply and put his arm around his son. Together they trudged towards the tower heads set against the cold wind.

The girls and Sybil headed towards the shops to see what was interesting there.

"I have to get tee-shirts for all my cousins, and perhaps some curios for my aunt."

"I am sure we will find something," Sybil answered. She felt like taking Alicia's hand, but didn't quite dare. There was something aloof about her in spite of her friendliness. It was as if she was actually afraid of being touched, as if her carefully assembled sense of self would disintegrate or perhaps melt at the intimate warmth of a human hand.

Andrea skipped along happily, feeling quite in her element. She was oblivious of the strong undercurrent between the two older women. They desperately wanted to be friends—with hearts open to each other, but simply didn't know how. However they managed to spend a happy time looking for shirts that would be just right for the different personalities back in Kenya.

Up in the tower, John and his son took in the breathtaking view of the falls below which even from up there looked gigantic.

"One day when you're a father you will know just how glad I am to have you here by my side today," John said to his son who was completely taken in by the breath-taking view.

"I'm not saying this to pressurise you into making

any decision," he continued. " Indeed I would be a fool not to recognise that you are a child of two worlds, and due to the way things have been and of course to the kind of temperament you have, you belong more to Africa, where hope is still young and strong in spite of everything fate and man have thrown at that continent. I just want you to know that to have you by my side makes me feel that I have not lived in vain, that somewhere along the way I did do something right."

"I'm glad to be here too, dad. And while I'm at it let me apologise for being such a silly ass back in Nairobi. I asked my aunt and uncle to explain a little bit more and I think I understand a little better. In any case Auntie pointed out that while none of us can ever change the past, our actions can so blaze today that the past will simply fade into oblivion."

"A wise woman, your aunt," John murmured and looked away at the rainbow curving over the falls.

Finally they made their way down to the agreed-upon rendezvous, but had to wait for quite a while before the ladies appeared laden down with parcels.

That night Sybil spoke to John about her inability to really reach Alicia,

"I really want her to know and feel that I am her friend, that I really care, but she is in constant control of her friendliness. Every statement is carefully thought out and weighed before it is uttered. I may be exaggerating but I think that she even considers what impact she will make before she laughs. She just doesn't let herself go. It's unnatural."

179

"Take it easy, sweet-heart. She has had to travel a long road to reach here. And maybe it is not for you to thaw her out. She is very fair in her judgement of people and I am sure she knows that you are genuine. All you can do is be there for her when she needs you."

"But you know me—impetuous is my middle name. I want to act, to love, to show some emotion, for heavens sake!"

"One other thing you must know is that Kenyans are a particularly reticent people. It is considered bad form to show your feelings in public or even too much of it in private. They are very much in control of their emotions. The fact that they were colonised by the British for three-quarters of a century did nothing to improve that national characteristic."

"But she is Canadian too."

"That is what I hope she will learn, belated though it is, and you are a damned good teacher, I must say. Look at what a yelp our daughter is." She punched him on the side.

"That's not fair. That child takes after you! Besides she was born yelling—it's just her personality."

"I wasn't complaining. Andrea will not wait for life to happen, she will make it happen. If man was made to create and be creative, then she is the perfect specimen. In any case don't worry about Alicia. As sure as I live, she is a blossom that is just waiting for the right touch and then you will not be able to believe the magnificence of her bloom."

But Sybil was so dissatisfied with the whole problem of Alicia, that one day she called up her brother Brett and told him to come over for the weekend,

"There is a young lady I want you to meet."

"Look here, sis!" Brett protested, "the last young lady you wanted me to meet turned out to be a perfect idiot. Believe me, I can manage my life without your help. I'm no longer fifteen you know."

"Listen, you ass," Sybil retorted. She was very thankful that she and her siblings were very close and quite familiar with each other. Besides she rested in the knowledge of their firm affection and admiration. "This is not like anything you imagine; you are required here strictly in the role of chaperone and your entire approach must be avuncular. You know about my step-daughter from Africa who is visiting with us."

Yes, Brett knew all about her step-daughter from Africa. But he had been warned not to show his face anywhere near the vicinity unless and until requested. Sybil had wanted a free hand with her step-children until such a time that she was confident of the relationship. She was horrified at the possibility of being cast into the role of a wicked step-mother. This lack of confidence was so atypical that Brett, who lived quite nearby in Toronto and would have loved to meet John's children, was taken aback and amused at the same time.

"Why this sudden change of policy?" he asked, laughing.

"Don't laugh, you dolt. The matter is deadly

serious. I've already bought two tickets for the concert by the *Toronto Philharmonic* to which you should graciously invite her. You will be at your most attentive and well behaved—the perfect uncle, get it?"

"No I don't *get it* sis, but I'll do anything to help you out." And he meant it.

So Professor Brett Stanley turned up punctually for lunch at his sister's house in Brampton. He was of medium height, rather slim of build, with an angular jaw, vivid blue eyes and a dark mop of hair atop a tanned face. For all intents and purposes he had just dropped in casually. A place was rapidly laid out for him and he proceeded to make himself the soul of the gathering. He had a repertoire of stories from every corner of the globe and was a brilliant conversationalist, the epitome of a man of the world. Johnny took to him immediately and the two were soon swapping tall yarns about life on campus.

At first Alicia showed no reaction at all at this sudden intrusion of a young, good looking and highly attractive male. She was a past mistress at ignoring men who had high opinions of themselves, as she tried to convince herself Brett no doubt had. But apart from a general vague look in her direction once or twice, he appeared not to notice her existence, which, she tried to convince herself, suited her very well.

Johnny was soon calling him by his Christian name while Alicia continued to refer to him chillingly as Professor Stanley.

"Call me Brett," he drawled, brilliant blue eyes resting on her momentarily. "Nobody believes I'm a real professor you know." Everybody laughed and Alicia would have felt like a little girl except for the impact of that casual look which made her feel so entirely like a woman. Confused she looked quickly away even though he was already looking elsewhere.

"What is Linguistics anyway?" Johnny asked intrigued by the phenomenon of so young a professor, though he himself had moved in academic circles all his life. However, he realised that medicine was essentially different from other lines of knowledge in that it was highly focused—its boundaries rigidly drawn by the perimeter of the human body, diseased or healthy. When dealing with matters of life and death, where a three minutes delay meant the difference between a living brain and a dead one, the mind had to be trained in snappy thinking. There really was no room for the intellect to roam. This of course had drawbacks.

"Linguistics, loosely put, is the study of the nature of language as an expression of thought. Language in turn is the oral or written expression of a concept which first exists in the mind. There cannot be language unless the idea first exists in the mind."

"Do you speak many languages then?" Johnny asked, quite missing the point.

"I do, but that is entirely coincidental. In any case every Canadian student is supposed to study at least two languages, French and English, by law. Linguistics, however, has got nothing to do with learning languages as such; rather, it has to do with the nature of language as a vehicle for communicating thought."

"Huh?" said Johnny with a comical look on his face.

Not a man to be carried away with self-importance, Brett just laughed and said,

"I agree. It does sound rather airy, nothing like the solid meat of Medicine." Johnny had the grace to laugh at the magnitude of his ignorance. Alicia said nothing. The man made her feel awkward and afraid. But of what? He had hardly looked in her direction the whole afternoon. She who had never bothered about her looks suddenly felt a strong desire to wear something attractive. But what did she care? She wasn't interested in him.

"Look here, Johnny my man. How would you like to go with me to a concert I particularly want to see? Then I'll take you out for a drink and show you Toronto by night. The concert will be by the *Toronto Philharmonic*."

Sybil held her breath. She had not thought that Brett would ask *Johnny* out! What was the idiot up to?

"That sounds great, but I'm not one for concerts and things. Besides dad and I are going to watch a ball game this afternoon and just talk about things, you know. We really don't have that much time together. But my sister is crazy about music, why don't you take her? I'm sure she would be delighted." All eyes turned to Alicia, who prayed for an earthquake to come and bury them all, beginning with Johnny.

"Would you like to come?" Brett asked smiling at her absently.

"Of course," she heard herself saying, much to her amazement. She smiled uncertainly at him, her eyes unveiled and unprotected. Brett was arrested and held in suspense by those eyes. Suddenly this became, not a game, but a deadly serious business. They looked at each other, and Sybil's alert antennae picked up the electricity between them.

"*Uncle Brett*," she said in her sweetest voice, "please don't forget to bring some chocolate for Andrea, you know how she loves them."

It was Brett's turn to say "Huh?" Not once had his gifts of chocolate been acknowledged publicly. He sneaked them to Andrea on the sly and had not known that her mother knew. Sybil glared at him;

"I hope you will be a better uncle now than you have been in the past." Brett finally got the message and nodded vigorously.

"Of course, sis, of course!"

Alicia asked to be excused and went to her room to agonise over what to wear. Finally she settled on the only dressy thing she had, a graceful waist-hugging pale coral dress that Wandia had given her practically at gun-point back in Nairobi. She rushed to Sybil's bathroom, sprayed on some perfume and put some colour on her lips. Thus armoured, she made a reappearance in the sitting-room. There was a little silence. Then Brett, ignoring Sybil, said,

"You look lovely."

"Thank-you." And with a proprietorial air, Brett marched her out of the room.

"Take care," Sybil almost wailed after them, wondering whether she had done the right thing after all. She got no answer. *If anything happens to her, her aunt would kill me.*

John, who had silently observed the little by-play between Sybil and Brett, smiled understandingly at Sybil's distracted look.

"Don't worry so much. Alicia is after all twenty-four years old and knows what she wants. And Brett's a very nice guy. I am her father and I am not unduly worried."

"What do *you* know?" she answered and abruptly left the room. Johnny looked from one to the other wondering what the matter was. He had missed everything. The two settled down to watch the ball game.

After having yelled to their hearts content for over one hour, John suggested a walk. Even though it was only five, it was almost dark. Johnny still had to get used to the sight of the 'dying' trees. He was used to tropical evergreens.

"Do you think you could ever live here?"

"I suppose out of dire necessity, yes: but I am Kenyan dad, it is the place which calls to my heart and where I feel that all is well with me."

"A bright lad like you would have a tremendous opportunity here."

"I know that, dad, and that the pay is lousy back home in Kenya. And that here, they would treat me with the respect I deserve as a professional; that I would never have to do a ward-round in a ward where the only plentiful commodity are the patients strewn all over the floor and every available space. But do you know that each time a patient goes home well despite all the odds—few drugs, broken down equipment, not even enough of the bare necessities—I will feel that I have served those who really need it, but can never hope to pay, but then again, who can really pay the price of restored health?"

"But wouldn't you like to make money?"

"Plenty of it. All my dreams are staked on the fact that I will have plenty of money."

"But how?"

"There are many people who could pay for their healthcare. I will have no compunction in charging fees from these. But there are all kinds of miserable little people who become sick and die in their villages without the faintest hope of seeing a doctor or getting to hospital, and if they do, they are likely to be sold, with their families and whatever little property they have—to meet the bills."

John shook his head and then said:

"I have arranged with a friend of mine who runs an aviation school to take you on from Monday."

"That's wonderful. But dad, nothing will make me change my mind about going back, though I'll be back to visit you and Sybil from time to time. I like her very much.

"I'm not trying to bribe you, son. I know how you feel. I myself had wanted to make Kenya my home when your mother and I were still together. Let's go back home. Your aunt gave me something that I think you would like to listen to." He suddenly sounded very mysterious and Johnny looked at him suspiciously, but the older man turned on his heel and started to walk rapidly back. Johnny had no choice but to do the same.

As they passed under the awning of a café, three white, burly-looking youths approached them and crowded them in. Suddenly one dug a painful elbow into Johnny's ribs. Johnny sprang back thinking that they were muggers, but the boys started laughing uproariously. It was, however, the boys' unlucky day for apart from studying Medicine, Johnny was more than just a passably good karateka and worked-out twice a week. Like an uncoiling spring he lashed out at the nearest boy with a flying kick and pivoting in mid-air landed lightly on his feet ready for a second attack. The boy lay sprawled on the pavement. His friends, feeling unequal to the situation, took to their heels.

"Are you ok?" John asked in a shaken voice. He was completely taken aback by the swiftness of the attack and counter-attack. Johnny was trembling with fury but was otherwise unhurt.

"What the hell was that about?" he asked, though the purpose of the attack was becoming clearer to him.

"I'm afraid," John said, feeling ashamed of the absurd attack, "that some people think that those who are not like them in every way, should be held in contempt. Of course, it only betrays their ignorance, bad manners and inferiority complex. I'm sorry."

"It's ok." But he resolved to be more watchful in future. The world was full of all kinds of bastards.

When they got home, John made straight for his den and taking a pretty ordinary looking cassette tape mounted it on an old-fashioned looking player.

"I've had this for over ten years," he boasted. Johnny could only agree —the machine looked prehistoric;

"Sure looks like it."

The golden voice of David Amunga came crooning out— thirty years or more before the advent of the likes of John Sigu Courtney;

> 'My life in America
> Such happy happy life
> But I am feeling loneliness
> When I remember Africa
>
> I'm going back to Kenya
> My home of happiness
> My people are crying for me
> So let me go back home!'

Johnny who had had an amused smile on his face at the beginning, could not even attempt to speak by the time the archaic piece of music ended.

"Yeah!" said Johnny finding his voice at last. "That's exactly what I meant. Thanks dad for understanding so well."

"I suppose we should thank your aunt Wandia for many things."

"Yes, that too." And he left and went to his room to be alone with his thoughts.

ELEVEN

ALICIA

OF ALL THE MASTERS of classical music, Alicia liked the work of that German genius, Wolfgang Amadeus Mozart, best of all. It seemed to her, especially today, that he took the longings of the human heart and wove them into ineffable music. But she had never been conscious of such unfettered joyousness in her life before—for as fate would have it, the Toronto Philharmonic was having a Mozart Night—almost as if they had known that she would be coming and that she would choose this very night in which to fall deeply in love with a man who was essentially a stranger. All through the evening, her heart trembled with emotion and music.

If Brett had set out on a seduction, he could hardly have chosen a better setting. But he had not, nor was he that kind of man. Whenever he felt like reaching out for her hand, a desire which was becoming more and more irresistible as the evening wore on, he had to do his instincts violence by reminding himself that he was here on trust as uncle and chaperone!

But I'm not her uncle! However he knew that Sybil would be very angry with him if he overstepped his boundaries. He had to think of a way to get the girl to see him of her own free will.

"When are you going back home?" he whispered urgently in her ear.

Home? It all seemed so far away. She almost told him that her home was right here with him. That she had been looking for a home all her life without knowing it, but that at last, thank God she had found it.

"In six weeks time," she said, her voice sounding unreal even in her own ears.

"Could we go out for a drink sometime?" Before she could answer, the orchestrated playing the opening notes of *Eine Kleine Nachtmusic* (a little night music) and her heart stilled. Moments passed as she listened raptly. He waited and became impatient. He, Brett Stanley, was in an agony of suspension. Against his better judgment he took her hand and repeated the question. Again she remained silent, and this time he could feel the tremor of her hand in his. And Alicia Courtney, suddenly becoming conscious of where she was and who she was with, took wild and terrified fright at what was happening to her. She snapped her hand out of his and face burning stared right ahead of her.

"Please take me home," she said in wooden tones.

"I'm sorry if I have offended you," he stammered. "I didn't mean any harm. I would never hurt you in any way." *Better to die myself,* he thought frantically.

"Please take me home," she repeated again as if all other words had been erased from her brain and only these four remained. She stood up and he had no choice but to get up too amid hisses of rage from the audience. As they made their way out he called himself every name under heaven— *you idiot, you nitwit, you numskull! You finally meet a girl worth knowing and you blow it, you! You!*

But home he had to take her. Sybil opened the door at the first ring as if she had camped next to it all evening. The smile froze on her face when she saw the look on Alicia's face. Wordlessly Alicia left them in the hall without an explanation.

"What did you do to her!" Sybil demanded glaring at her hapless brother.

"Nothing sis, you know I'm not such a goat. I just took her hand and she freaked out!"

"She is a highly sensitive person, don't you know!" And she would have banged the door on his face except for the queer look on his face.

"And what is the matter with you any way?"
He went round her and sat down heavily.

"I think I'm in love with Alicia and already she loathes the sight of me. Just for holding her hand, for heaven's sake."

"Well, don't go around holding people's hands

unless they ask you to," she said amused and exasperated at the same time.

"Please talk to her for me."

"Me? Never! You want her to include me in her nefarious characters' book along with you?"

"Oh come on, sis!"

"Why don't you go back home and accept that Alicia is least interested?"

He groaned and stood up to leave. Relenting a little, she added, "I suggest you leave her alone for a while— a long while even. This is no ordinary girl. If you attempt pursuit in the usual manner, you will lose her forever and perhaps do a lot of damage as well."

"God forbid!"

She laughed outright, enjoying his predicament.

"It is so heartwarming to know that you can actually care about someone other than yourself."

"Oh get off my case!" Bret stumbled out of the door. In truth she loved him best of all her siblings. He was open and warm-hearted and just about the most dependable brother a person could have. And she knew for a fact that he avoided the undergraduate girls—who threw themselves at him in hordes—like the very plague, and this must have taken a lot of will power. He was such an attractive man. She hoped that Alicia would soon come to her senses.

The following one week was filled with tension. Brett seemed to spend every waking moment on the phone trying to get a chance to talk to Alicia, who would have none of it, but she gave no explanation as to why she wouldn't talk to him or what had transpired on the fateful night. The following Saturday afternoon, Brett arrived in person. Alicia took one look, fled to her bedroom and refused to come out. It soon became clear that she would be dislodged by nothing short of a fire brigade.

"I strongly advise you to leave her alone. She has made it more than clear that she does not want to associate with you," Sybil said and John concurred. In fact the two were afraid that the young lady might simply get up and fly away before the visit was over.

"But listen John, I love your daughter. I can't even begin to imagine how I can continue living without her."

"You were doing quite well two weeks ago," John said, tongue-in-cheek.

"You call that life? I was one of the walking dead. I am alive now."

"Perhaps too alive," was Sybil's rejoinder. "I suggest you go back to your old life and consider many things that I'm sure you haven't thought of. For example that more than anything else she is an African with an African's way of looking at things. She probably found your entire way of behaving reprehensible in ways that a dolt like you could not even begin to understand—"

"But I was at my better than best! Remember I was supposed to behave like an uncle!"

"Some uncle!"

"What is this?" John demanded, sensing that something was being kept from him.

Sybil glared at her brother and then smiling said to her husband,

"Nothing, just a joke between Brett and myself."

Brett, however, did not look like he was enjoying himself at all. John, feeling sorry for him, said,

"Go back home, old chap. I think you need to go back to the drawing board and think up a new approach."

Back in her room Alicia's mind was in turmoil. She had had a bad week trying to forget Mozart and Brett who had somehow become inextricably mixed up in her head. She wished that she was far away in Africa where she hoped she could forget him, but at the same time she longed to see him just once more before she left—his wide smiling eyes and surprisingly gentle face. She wanted to hold his hand again, just one more time; and to sit near him again—of course just one more time! And then she would just naturally forget him—if she could only put a few thousands of miles between them. But she had behaved so childishly that she knew he wouldn't come, surely he was used to more sophisticated women?

So when he had unexpectedly turned up—like an answer to a prayer, like a cherished dream taking flesh, it was just too much. Her heart leapt so wildly at the sight of him that she had to flee to protect herself from going to him involuntarily. In her room she had to face the fact that she loved him. And she wept. For what, after all, did she have to offer a man like that? He would soon discover that she was timid and lacked confidence, and that she was afraid of giving herself for fear that she would be hurt. Besides she was of mixed race in a race-conscious world. Surely would this be a stumbling block sooner than later? She did not have the strength to fight off a lifetime of innuendoes.

Sybil knocked once and came into the room. Alicia blew her nose and quickly wiped her eyes but there was no hiding the fact that she had been weeping. Sybil said nothing. She stood by the window in a characteristic posture, studying the world in all its variable and sometimes severe beauty. Today it was dark and forbidding with a sultry sky and a whipping wind that drove the skeletal trees in a wild lopsided dance. A fitting background for this poor fearful child with a woman's beautiful body and a child's night-time terrors. So long did the silence become that Alicia finally felt obliged to make an attempt at a feeble explanation.

"I am sorry, but I'm not very used to men." Sybil looked at her tenderly, but only beckoned. Alicia went to stand by her side. For a long time the two women stood looking at nature flexing her muscles.

A man was coming out of a doorway across the street. He was buttoned to the chin and body bent forward he lurched into the wind, his coats flapping behind him.

"Sometimes even though it is dark and the wind appears rough, you must walk into the wind. One cannot postpone life or avoid it altogether. If you do you die anyway. And to die from an unlived life is an unforgivable sin. I believe those are the only people who go to hell straight, with no court of appeal. Sometimes the sky is bright and you feel like dancing on air. Sometimes the sky is dark and you must grope in the dark. No matter, just keep moving, even if you appear to be making very little progress. If you stop moving you die."

Alicia digested this in silence and then said, "I love him."

"No you don't, but *he* loves you—perhaps because he is older and therefore knows what he wants. You on the other hand are walking on air. He thrills you. He has awoken the woman in you and that makes your heart and body tremble. It's a heady feeling, never to be missed and never to be repeated. But a moment will come when you will look into the quiet places of your heart and you will discover that he is you and you are him. The moment comes when both of you will have already caused each other to shed tears of blood. For most of us in our folly, this is the only way. You have already caused him to shed such tears, while you weep here out of pure self-pity. To the best of my knowledge, self-pity and self-love tend to go together, but it's got very little to do with loving another person."

"That's not true, I love him!" Alicia's face, usually so self contained, was burning with affront and disbelief. But because she was a very honest person and quite capable of clear-headed unmuddled thinking, she paused and glanced into her heart. And like a dream the years of her life passed before her—the silent little girl she had been, not so much caught up in her own world as shutting others out of it. The self-contained adolescent and young adult she had become, disdaining others with their rank and uncontrolled emotions. She had never opened herself to any one— no, not even to Wandia who was perhaps the only person she had ever trusted completely. She had been so caught up in the drama of her own personal tragedy as to be unaware of anyone else's needs. And this strange woman, her stepmother, had unerringly put her finger on this flaw in her personality.

"He left you a note," Sybil said, handing it over. And then she left the room.

Alicia took the note gingerly as if it might bite. She was more afraid of what it might contain than she had ever been afraid of anything else in her entire life. She toyed with the idea of destroying it without reading it, and then to walk away to her old undisturbed existence. But her aunt had said that if you stopped moving you died. What would she say of someone who not only stopped moving, but was actually moving backwards? Decomposing perhaps. Finally she opened the letter and found that her hands were trembling as she pulled out the single sheet of note paper.

Dear Alicia,

I have tried in vain to contact you. However your behaviour, today finally convinced me just how deeply I must have offended you. I suppose that there is nothing I can say to mitigate my case in your eyes, but all the same I want you to know that I am truly sorry. I also want you to know that somewhere in the world there is someone who will always fervently hope that you are happy wherever you will be.

All the very best
Brett.

That was all. Alicia Courtney shed tears. Then she sat down to write a note of her own. She tore it and wrote another one which she destroyed too. Finally she settled on,

Dear Brett,

Thank you for your note, but there is really nothing to forgive. I panicked, that's all. You did nothing to offend me at all. I have thought things over and I really would like us to get together again. I'll be waiting for your call.
And she dared sign it,

Affectionately
Alicia.
PS: The Toronto Philharmonic were lovely. I enjoyed them very much.

She eagerly went in search of Sybil to get Brett's address.

"Address?" Sybil asked , a strange look on her face.

"Yes," Alicia answered, her eyes shining with excitement and unconcealed joy. The customary shadows were missing from their depths. "I want to send him a note."

"But I'm afraid that's impossible."

"Why?" Alicia asked, but she was still smiling, not really believing that contacting Brett could be such a hustle.

"Apparently he has resigned from Toronto University and wants to take up a job in Switzerland, I'm not sure exactly where though. That's why he so desperately wanted to see you today."

"But he can't have left the country! It's only been a couple of hours since he was here!"

"No he has not left the country. He was going to spend a few days with a friend of his in Montreal. Unfortunately he didn't leave his address. I suppose it didn't occur to him that *you* would be wanting to contact him so urgently."

Sybil was sorry to see the shadows coming back thick and fast as Alicia turned away wordlessly and went back to her room. She was tempted to follow her but realised that some pains had to be borne alone. And the pain of becoming a woman was most definitely in that category.

Alicia suffered. Her life had only one focal point,

Brett. She played and replayed the short period of time they had spent together and in her imagination she amended every silly thing she had said or done. But of course it was too late. *I am a fool and I have always been one,* she said viciously to herself, but it didn't make it any better. Brett was a brilliant and very presentable man. Any intelligent woman could have seen this and would have snapped him up. It was unlikely that she would get another chance. Besides, with his proficiency in languages he would be at home lecturing anywhere in the world, while she herself wasn't even sure what language one spoke in Switzerland. In any case what made her think that he would be *that* interested in her?

A few phone calls could surely not be construed as signs of deep attachment? Who was she fooling?

After a week of this mental torture, Alicia confidentially told Sybil that she could not stand it any more. She wanted to go back home.

"But your father would be shattered and your brother is right in the middle of his flying lessons!"

"I'm sorry about dad, but I am sure he will understand if you explain everything to him—that I feel a fool, that I'm angry with myself, that I need time to recover—but not here where I'm so close yet so far from Brett, and that the best place for me to be for the time being is home, on familiar ground.

"As for Johnny, I see no reason why he shouldn't stay as long as he wants. It's strange, but it was I who wanted so badly to come and it was Johnny who was doubtful about the whole business. Now he has a wonderful relationship with dad, and he is doing things he has always wanted to do."

"Let me tell you outright that I'm a bit afraid of the strength of your feelings, that is you and Brett, for each other, and the rapidity with which it has developed. I myself am chary of such strong emotions. They tend to cloud up issues—such as the fact that you don't know each other well at all. So this separation may in itself be a good thing.

"Another thing is that you are looking at this from a very narrow and self-centered point of view. However madly in love you happen to be, remember that there are other people in your life who care and who also love you in different ways, that is unless you fell from heaven full-grown like the Greek goddess, Athene.

"You may fall in love or you may fall out of love, or whatever else life throws at you, and these people will be there praying and rooting for you, perhaps your father more than any other because he started so late and is guilt-ridden as a result. He says little but he wants with all his heart that your visit here be a great success. And believe me when I say that he is a very good man. Good enough for me to want to have another child with though I can tell you outright that I never planned for my life to include a child, let alone two! But I suppose we all must adjust the compass as we go along—which I can also tell you is what love is about—that is accommodating the needs of the other person.

"I appeal to that famous African generosity that so impressed your father during his visit—please don't leave now. It is sometimes a great virtue to keep people we love ignorant of certain things the knowledge of which would break them or at least wound them terribly and in this case even reverse certain great gains that have been made.

"Just think. It is in his house that you have found misery instead of happiness. It is not his fault, but he will think that once again he has let you down. It is in the nature of fathers to want to protect one from everything, even life itself—if they could. But no one can protect you from life indefinitely, though I must admit your aunt and uncle had a good go.

"You and Brett may or may not get together again. Nothing, after all, has been said, no promises given. But your father loves you and needs your affection. I beg you, please stay. A woman has to have staying power. It will stand you in good stead a thousand times over."

Alicia stayed.

As for Brett, it was as if he had left planet earth and had moved on into space.

TWELVE

ANTHONY SIGU

IT WAS MARK Oloo Sigu's great day. It wasn't every day that a fellow turned three in the midst of his family, extended family and over-extended family. There was every shade and hue of the Mugos, his mother's family, and an amazing number of people bearing that name which he had hitherto imagined belonged only to his big brother. Every other adolescent male seemed to be named Mugo, in the best Kikuyu tradition, where something as important as a name was not left to the mere whim of the two ecstatic parents, but rigidly determined by centuries-old tradition.

Accordingly, the first male born of a legal union was always named after his paternal grandfather, never mind what kind of a person the old goat may be. The second son was like-wise named after his maternal grandfather. The first daughter was named after her paternal grandmother and the second after the maternal, no doubt as a consolation to the mother, possibly to prevent another coup, for the Kikuyu, according to legend, had once been a matrilineal people with women being preeminent over men. Men, the legend goes, naturally did not take this lying down and decided to overthrow the yoke of women from their shoulders by using the nefarious method of making all their wives pregnant at the same time, a feat which no doubt must have required some master-strategists to plan and execute.

To support the at least partial authenticity of the legend, all the Kikuyu clans derive their names from the nine daughters of Gikuyu and Mumbi, the first Kikuyu man and woman who had received the decree to go forth and conquer from none other than Ngai, god of Mount Kirinyaga, the mountain of light—now known by the lesser name of Mount Kenya. The way they acquired husbands to procreate with is, of course, another great legend in itself.

To Mark's birthday also came all the Sigu clan who were not bed-ridden, maimed or in an Intensive Care Unit somewhere. For, you see, it was *Mzee's* (the old man's) big day, for Mark in his turn had been named after old Mark Anthony Oloo Sigu—though the Luo exercise the greatest latitude in the naming of children and depend for this, on dreams, visions or the mere *fiat* of the parents. For example, a Luo child may be quite authentically named Diego Maradona, Nelson Mandela, Diana Spencer, Morning (*Akinyi*), Evening

(Adhiambo), Night *(Atieno)* or other more traditional ancestral names, such as Oloo or Odero. It all depended on the inclination of his parents.

"They are all here because of me?" asked Mark in round-eyed wonder. He had not realised that he was such an important little person. The place was absolutely awash with cousins except for Johnny and Alicia. And there were at least four other fellows named Mark— *just like him!*

"Yes," his mother answered him. "To be alive is a very good thing, and you, my boy, are just about as alive as any one I've ever met. I mean you are absolutely full of it."

"I am?" He wasn't quite sure what he was supposed to be full of, but if his mother thought so, then no doubt, he was full of it.

"Yeap. Also your father wanted to get the family together again. It's been a long time since we all came together just to enjoy each other's company."

Mark understood the meaning even if he did not understand the words. He gave a whoop and making up his mind to enjoy himself thoroughly, raced into the garden to wrestle with several other Marks and a few Mugos; and to gaze with wonder at budding female mystiques which went by names such as Wangeci and Awiti. Even at three, Mark guessed that the female were a species unto themselves—and therefore to be treated with caution.

He ran full tilt into a man in a black shirt and a collar and was lifted up high. It was Uncle Father Tony.

"Hi, son!"

"Hi, uncle!" Mark giggled in pure undiluted high spirits. Then before the conversation could progress further, one of the younger Mugos stuck out his tongue at Mark. Such a challenge could not be taken lying down. Mark wriggled out of his uncle's arms and gave chase. The two little boys disappeared behind a clump of bougainvilleas.

Father Tony had been deep in conversation with a tall lanky young man who at fifteen stood an inch taller than the priest. It was Mugo Sigu. He was in the middle of classic teenage rebellion and had switched off from his family and seemed to spend a considerable amount of time with a group of adolescent boys, who, to put it mildly, looked highly shady and were apparently responsible to no-one.

One of them was the son of very wealthy neighbours of the Sigus and Wandia knew to a certainty that he had had problems with drugs and had been expelled from more than one school. If his parents had not been so well connected, he would most probably have been in an approved school, hopefully learning how to make an honest living. As it was, he was at home enjoying the easy life while his parents tried to figure out what next to do with him.

This boy had latched himself onto Mugo and seemed to have a powerful influence on him. Wandia and Aoro were afraid of making a move that would alienate their son who had been a perfectly normal boy before the unholy alliance had been forged.

208

They appealed to Father Tony who was known to have a way with boys, and apparently the tougher the better. The priest chose the natural occasion of Mark's birthday to strike up a conversation with his nephew. Mugo was on the defensive. Everybody knew Father Tony with his lucid and incisive mind. He could make one's heart stand still with one well reasoned and apparently irrelevant statement and seemed to combine both deep understanding of human nature, and of practical living in such a way that one could almost never wriggle out of coming face to face with oneself. Father Tony was never hazy; he was a man you wanted to avoid if you had a bad conscience that you did not want anyone to interfere with.

When Mugo saw him headed in his direction, he tried to slip behind the jacaranda. The priest bore down on him inexorably. Mugo had almost completed a three-hundred and sixty degree turn around the tree, with its gnarled trunk digging painful holes into his back, when Fr. Tony finally stood squarely in front of him.

"God should have made these trees a bit larger, don't you think? As it is they hardly provide a boy with any protection."

"Yes uncle. I mean, no, uncle!" The boy looked so sheepish that Tony burst out into characteristic gales of laughter.

"Come on, old chap. This is your uncle Tony! Surely you were not trying to avoid *me?*"

" 'Course not, uncle!" He shuffled his feet and tried

to look at his uncle, but his eyes shifted to a patch of grass, somewhere to the left of the Jacaranda. He studied this so intently that one would have thought that his next Biology paper would be on the subject of lawn grasses.

"Ah, I can see that I'm not very welcome." Fr. Tony turned and moved away rapidly but Mugo bounded after him and was beside him in two steps.

" 'Course you are welcome, uncle. Actually I really wanted to talk to you." Mugo was greatly surprised to hear himself utter that statement. It was as much news to him as it was to Fr. Tony. He had until that very moment believed that the very last *Homo Sapiens* a fellow in his position wanted to see was one who wore a dark shirt and a collar, especially if it went by the name of Fr. Anthony Sigu, his father's brother, who was known to say the kind of things which might cause severe damage to a boy's new-found freedom.

"You did?" said Fr. Tony sounding not very surprised. People wanted to talk to him who didn't even know it. And apparently the more they needed and wanted to talk to him the more they seemed not to know it.

Mugo rushed into his story headlong, as if he had been dying to get it off his chest.

"Actually, I'm hurting no-one uncle. I just hang out with these fellows, you see. Otherwise everybody will think that I am sissy or something. Guys in school were talking, see. They think I'm a book-worm or

210

something 'cause I get good grades and am at the top of the class most of the time. So I decided to hang out with the toughest of them all. I mean Git is a mean chap and anyone seen with him is obviously tough. But now he says that if I don't start smoking weed, they'll kick me out. I mean, cigarettes are for girls, don't you see?"

"What kind of animal is this *Git*?"

"Git's short for Gitau. He lives in that huge house down the road. And he has lots and lots of money. I really don't know where he gets it from because I know for sure his parents have refused to give him any money."

"You must really love this Git chap."

"*I hate him!*" Mugo hissed.

"So why hang out with a chap you don't even like?"

"You see, the guys at school...."

"You've already told me about the guys at school. Think of a better reason why an intelligent boy like you would want to so hurt a mother such as you have. There must be a better reason other than a lot of spineless guys at school."

Mugo thought. His mind drew a blank, so Fr. Tony decided to help him.

"Try spineless and see how it fits; or simply lacking spunk and personality; or too cowardly to be your own man. To be exactly like everybody else must look very desirable at fifteen. Like peas in a pod, like maize on a cob, like sheep in a pen. Exactly the same kind of idiot everyone else is. I myself can't think of anything more boring. Every morning I wake up and I say to myself, I'm a new man and it's a new day. I must try to be better than I was yesterday, for who knows, this may be the very last day I have to improve myself, to be better than I ever was.

"Have you ever stopped to ask yourself why you are not a street-child, hustling every day simply to keep soul and body together? What exactly did you ever do to deserve all that you have?"

He paused in midstep and swung towards the boy. His eyes were mere slits in his dark face. Mugo felt trapped under the intensity of that gaze.

"Nothing," he stammered. If he had ever thought anything at all, it was that the street children and other unfortunate people of that type were just there, a part of the landscape, unchangeable as the mountains, constant as the earth upon which he stood. In short, they were none of his business. He was entirely wrapped up with the exciting business of being fifteen years old and of exploring the edges of danger to see how far you could go before something exploded in your face. And of late he had been whirling away so fast, too afraid to stop and look into himself.

"*You* have been given much and much will be expected of you, my boy. You have already wasted a good fifteen years of your life, during which your ambition was only apparently to be like everybody else, disdaining the intelligence that has been given to you and, what is more, the chance to develop it. Believe me there are many equally or more intelligent boys who would give an arm and a leg to get the opportunities you have. You are not as smart as you think, by the way. I know any number of really bright boys who have no opportunity to develop their brains at all. You, on the contrary, have that opportunity.

"Stretch your brain, son. Hone your mind with study, make it a disciplined instrument to serve you. Take care of your body, it is the receptacle for your mind and spirit. Nothing except that which is beneficial and good should ever deliberately go into it.

"There is work to be done, my boy, and few the men who can do it. In this life you are either a leader or you are led. So be it. But it is a terrible crime for a man who could and should be a leader, to go into the pen and start bleating like a sheep. But then sheep are notoriously alike—so perhaps that is after all the right place for a man who wants to be exactly like everybody else."

It was at this point that young Mark had cannon-balled into his uncle. The interlude gave Mugo a minute in which to consider the depths to which he had sunk. He didn't like it. He, a bleating sheep! Never!

After young Mark had departed as suddenly as he had arrived, the man turned and looked at the boy again. Sadly he shook his head and, sighing, said,

"I had hoped for so much from you. I'm truly disappointed." With that he turned and walked away.

Mugo could have committed *harakiri* right there and then if that would not have caused even further disappointment in his already disappointed elder. He collapsed on the grass and began a serious review of his life.

Fr. Tony heard the sound of childish singing and headed in its direction. Wandia, with the help of her sister-in-law, Jael, had gathered the younger members of the clan around a large cake.

"And here is uncle Fr. Tony himself to bless the cake!" she sang. Tony immediately got into the spirit of the occasion and declared;

"Lord, bless this wonderful cake, and bless the children who will eat it so that they can grow tall and wise, but always funny!"

"Amen!" And all fell to with appetites driven by youth and the excellent weather.

With the children preoccupied, Wandia and Fr. Tony got into serious conversation. Jael, realising that the two needed to talk, waved them off and went on serving the children.

"Tell me the worst. Is he on drugs?" The priest, who was by nature and long training a tactful and careful person, could not help but burst into gales of laughter at this evidence of misplaced parental anxiety. But then again if he himself had been the parent of a fifteen-year-old boy who was hanging out with the neighbourhood thugs, he would probably have been even more anxious. Wandia relaxed immediately at the sound of his mirth. Sane people don't normally laugh at the face of impending catastrophe, and Tony was a very sane person.

"Come on, sis! Give the boy some credit for at least basic intelligence. Now there is an excellent young man if I ever saw one."

"Do I know whom you are talking about?"

"The same."

"Oh!"

"Listen, sis." She suddenly realised that he had never called her anything but *sis* since the day she married his brother. She understood that it allowed him to be personal without being intimate, approachable without clouding the fact that even from her, he was a man set apart.

"It would be abnormal if a boy that age did not attempt to be his own man. All of us have to forge our independence from the thickest and most necessary of bonds, the parental bond. Our early attempts to break free may sometimes appear foolish and even dangerous, but break free we must—it is a necessary condition of achieving adulthood.

"You are very lucky because what he has actually rebelled about is not your value system, but rather the fact of his own excellence. I have a strong suspicion that the boy realises that more will be asked of him than from the great majority, and therefore he is apprehensive. His response is to try and blend into the faceless crowd where he hopes he might be passed over as just another faceless body. In any case, don't worry, but pray that you will have the strength and generosity to support him when he stops running and stands still— to listen."

Wandia was silent for a very long time. She understood immediately what Tony was alluding to. Finally all she could utter was a small "Oh!" at the end of a deep sigh. *It seems that in this generation too at least one of them will be called away. How strange!* And she was surprised to discover that now she was more apprehensive than ever. *Surely not her son! Why should he be singled out of the crowd? The other one was dead, why should this one be taken away too? Didn't God have any other places to look?*

And then she was ashamed of herself and her thoughts. Abruptly she excused herself from Tony, who was looking at her with sympathetic understanding. She headed towards her study to sort out her confused thoughts.

Left to his own devices so suddenly, Tony shook his head slightly and decided to look for the rest of the clan who were on the opposite side of the house grilling meat, chicken, sausage and any hoofed or two winged thing that had not had the foresight to decamp to safer territory. Apart from all the Mugos of both sexes, their spouses and older children, Aoro was there with his twin brothers Odongo and Opiyo Sigu and their wives, as well as their little sister Mary, who had been the beloved child of Mark and Elizabeth Sigu's old age. Mary was now married with two children of her own.

There was a lull in the conversation as Fr. Tony rounded the corner. He had this effect on people, it did not surprise him any more.

"I thought Catholic priests had long stopped wearing uniforms?" someone asked *sotto voce*.

Aoro, who was also used to the reaction answered without looking at the person who had asked the question;

"Not my brother. At all times he is a priest nor does he try or even want to hide this fact from any one. A priest for ever. That's my brother." There was great satisfaction, even pride in his voice. He raised his voice,

"Welcome! I was beginning to wonder what had become of you!"

"Ah well, I had to stop on the other side and do the very important business of blessing the cake. The children would have been disappointed if I had not given it the great importance it deserved." He settled down with a drink and gradually the conversation began a more natural ebb and flow again. Everyone soon realised that Anthony Sigu was a very well informed man, but he was fresh and simple and totally unaffected. Everyone was soon asking him, 'But father, don't you think...?'and listening to what he had to say. And what he had to say was well thought, well phrased and very logical.

After some time Wandia emerged to join the gathering, but it was only Tony who noticed that she was uncharacteristically silent. She went and sat by her sister Esther who was quite beside herself with the fact that she had recently become a grandmother. She beamed at Wandia and continued the conversation where she had left it off sometime earlier;

"And the little one is so pretty, an angel I promise you. And she is so clever! She can already hold up her head at two months! And of course her name is Esther Wambui. Isn't that a lovely name for a little girl?" Her sister's good-hearted joy was infectious. Wandia laughed and said,

"Of course! It is the prettiest name in the world—after all it is the name of my only sister!"

Both sisters laughed together. A child is a good thing and always invested with hope.

FOURTEEN

A MATTER OF LOVE

ALICIA AND JOHN had been back home for a while and life at the Sigu household appeared to have gone back to the more normal upheavals of daily life.

Mark was in kindergarten from where he acquired an endless collection of *new* things to tell his mother whom he considered totally ignorant and in need of information as seen and understood by her loving and concerned son, Mark.

"Teacher said that this shape is called a *tri-gangle*," he would announce with dogmatic authority.

"Not a *triangle*?" Wandia would inquire mildly.

"No! A tri-gangle!" but she knew from past experience that *teacher said* would be words that a mere mother like herself could not argue with for a long time to come. The teacher was the first social other that a child came into prolonged contact with away from the safety of his own home. She not only held the knowledge, but made demands upon a little person that perhaps no one else had ever done—such as having to sit still for more than one minute or asking for permission to go to the toilet. Just imagine that—permission to go to the toilet! Whoever heard of such a thing? Besides, your formerly all-powerful parents apparently had no power to remove you from the domain of the teacher except at times determined by the teacher herself. It was natural that a little person of some basic intelligence would sooner than later, light up on the idea that one could try to use the teacher's immense authority to back up one's own fragile one, especially when dealing with one's parents and their various peculiar demands such as that one eat peas.

"Teacher said that peas are very bad," Mark tried one day. He hated the ugly green things rolling around in his plate and liked to use them as missiles when no one was watching.

"Oh, she did?" Wandia asked with interest. "I must discuss this with her as soon as possible." Mark watched with horror as she got up, went to the phone and dialled a number. He did not realise that one finger was pressing down a button.

"Hello! Is that teacher Pamela?"

Pause.

"I'm glad I found you teacher. I hear you have been telling my son Mark that peas are very bad for him?"

Pause.

"You did not? He said it very clearly and he is a

very good boy. He does not tell lies." Pause. From the corner of her eye she saw Mark eating each and every pea and everything else on his plate at a hitherto unmatched speed.

"You mean you don't want him to come back to school if he is going to tell such lies?" At which point of the conversation Mark slunk away and went to take his afternoon nap without being prompted—which was surely a first in his entire life.

Mugo, who seemed to be growing like a weed, had broken off his friendship with *Git the tough,* but he seemed to find an alarming number of reasons to go out every Saturday to Fr. Tony's church, down in Kariobangi, where he, among other things, was teaching a group of boys from the slums how to play basketball, with the help of a Marist Brother called Francois (Franco for short) from Cote d'Ivoire and Fr. Tony when he had time. Mugo was surprised to discover that despite his lack of height, the priest was agile, fast and could leap like a Maasai. Bro. Franco proved to be very useful and spent part of every Saturday evening teaching him French with the result that he shot past the rest of his class in this previously weak area. For this at least his mother was grateful.

Soon the team was so good that Mugo went to his headmaster to ask whether they could play against his school, which had one of the best basketball teams of any school in the country. It would encourage the boys who had previously preferred football anyway—and considered basketball a bourgeois game, while any poor boy could play football. The headmaster, a straight-laced fellow if ever there was one, looked at Mugo as if he had gone crazy and declined the offer to have his boys play basketball against a ragtag team from the slums. So Mugo and Bro. Franco had to look elsewhere. *Who said it was meant to be easy?*

As for Johnny, he had taken to his books like one demented, determined to be the best flying doctor the entire continent had ever seen.

"When you are making a diagnosis in the middle of nowhere, you need to be a walking medical library," he had once remarked.

But Alicia was distracted and it soon became very clear to Wandia at least that something was seriously wrong. However, she would not talk. She went back to her work and studies with her usual dedication, but without the spirit that had previously animated at least this one aspect of her life. She had never been a very talkative person, but these days she seemed practically mute.

"But what is it?" Wandia asked Johnny after failing to get any useful answers out of her.

"I don't know," Johnny said genuinely perplexed.

"Was there a man she was interested in out there?"

"No, but Brett, that is Sybil's brother, was very interested in her. But that was entirely one sided—Alicia loathed him, and I mean absolutely loathed him."

"That *is* strange. She usually is quite indifferent to

the opposite sex. They leave her unmoved. Look how long Dr Ayaga, to mention just one person, has been trying to get her attention. And it is as if she doesn't even see him. Even Lisa is advanced in comparison—at least she reacts when some poor soul is misguided enough to show interest. But Alicia is simply unmoved. Very strange." But Alicia chose to keep her counsel, though her appetite was bad and she lost weight.

Suddenly, about six months after their return from Canada, Alicia started going out with someone. He never once came in but would honk for her from his car and she would go out to him. It became clear that Alicia was not about to invite him into the house. Johnny was dying of curiosity and one day, on the unknown man's fourth call, he slipped out through the kitchen door and hid himself in some shrubs. As Alicia came out, the hall light lit the man's face clearly. He did not come round to open the door for her but did it from inside his car.

"Rude brute," thought Johnny then he staggered indoors. His face was a study in disbelief.

"I just knew! I just knew that she would go and do something like this!" he groaned.

"Do what?" cried Wandia alarmed.

"The man Alicia's going out with is old enough to be her father!" Wandia relaxed.

"Johnny, if I remember correctly any one over thirty is very old as far as you are concerned."

"Believe me Auntie. The guy is really old. He is even grey."

"Grey and old don't always go together, Johnny, besides it's your sister's business who she goes out with. I don't remember her interfering with some of the very strange females you bring around here. Some of them are real cause for alarm."

"But I am never serious about them, while Alicia is usually serious about everything she does. Do something Auntie, please!" he begged.

"No, Johnny. When Alicia's ready she will tell us. She is twenty-five, you know, and of sound mind. Meanwhile we wait and try to be civilised about this."

"I doubt," said Johnny ominously.

"Doubt what, Johnny?" enquired his aunt beginning to get exasperated.

"That she is of sound mind!"

"Give it a break will you?" Johnny recognising that his aunt was determined not to interfere, did.

About three months after the advent of the unknown man Alicia informed her family that she would bring him home for lunch one Saturday. *At last!* was the general consensus. This was the first time in twenty-five years that this was going to happen. Everyone was on tenterhooks and Anwarite, for one, spent her time trying to teach her renegade brother, Gandhi, some rudiments of table manners.

"You're not supposed to chew so loudly!" she informed poor Gandhi.

"I don't!" he protested.

"You do. And you must eat with your mouth

closed!" Gandhi glared at her, but she went on relentlessly,

"And you don't lean halfway across the table to get something. You ask someone to pass it over." Gandhi dived at her.

"Now, now children," intervened Wandia.

The day finally came and every one tried not to gaze at the man in wonder and the woman who had found it fit to befriend him in even greater wonder. He wasn't that old—just some twenty years or so older than Alicia. He was fighting a lost battle with middle-age spread and was a career civil servant doing a nondescript job in a nondescript manner, though he seemed to have rather formidable connections. He was painstaking to the point of being pompous. His conversation seemed to consist of a combination of cliches and slogans. He was also very surprised that such a girl from such a family would look at him twice. Instead of making him feel humbled, which would at least have made him tolerable, it made him feel even more pompous. After all he had always suspected that he was quite an intelligent man and not bad looking, otherwise why did the girl agree to go out with him when he had asked her to without any hope of being given as much as the time of day?

He had gone to see her in his official capacity as Director of Culture and National Heritage, a job whose only requirement seemed to be that he organise quasi-traditional dancers from various corners of the country to entertain visiting dignitaries. He had heard that one of the schools she taught had won the recent Inter-school Music and Drama Festival with a rousing piece called 'The Dance of the New Moon'. Apparently no one had ever seen anything like it before.

He had been married once but the woman had departed with the one offspring of the union and the next thing he heard was that she had married someone else. Thereafter he couldn't work up a prolonged interest in any female—his life was pretty comfortable as it was. While his friends were hassling around for school fees, some idiot was raising his son for him while *he* enjoyed life!

Then along came Alicia, looking like a vision from another world. *Wasn't he a lucky man now?* She was way beyond anything he had ever imagined in his wildest dreams and he thought he was madly in love with her and she, of course, with him. The truth however was that Alicia couldn't care less and he himself was in love with the things going out with her did to his ego. He was quite certain that many of his friends were dying of envy and would have happily given him cyanide. Alicia, on the other hand, was desperately trying to exorcise Brett from her mind and this man was as harmless as any. Then she suddenly decided that she would marry him; after all what was she waiting for? She would ever only love Brett anyway and since she could never have him, what did it matter whom she married? This pompous ass was just as bad as anybody else. And that was when she decided to bring him home.

Alicia was not incapable of humour and the looks on the faces of her family when she introduced her 'boyfriend' made her want to laugh out loud.

"Uncle, auntie, please meet my friend Napoleon Lebulu. Leb, my uncle and aunt, Dr. and Professor, Aoro and Wandia Sigu." She knew such things impressed him just as she knew he would address her uncle as professor and her aunt as Mrs.

"Glad to meet you Professor. Glad to meet you Mrs. Sigu," he said shaking hands profusely. Nobody bothered to correct him—it would have required unnecessary and lengthy explanations to convince him that she was indeed a bonafide professor and that he was a doctor and that nobody minded at all one way or the other. So for the rest of the evening Aoro resigned himself to being addressed as Professor Sigu.

The man was effusive and dominated the table with all the latest cliches and appropriate political slogans. Everyone else just gazed at him in wonder. The only person who would have been equal to the situation was young Mark, but he had been fed early and dispatched to bed, a feat which his daddy had accomplished only after promising to buy him half the contents of the toy shops on Biashara Street. Of course, mummy would probably veto everything, but Mark knew, from the wisdom acquired from three years of active existence, that if you played your cards right and you found yourself alone with your daddy in front of a shop one day, you could gently remind him that on such and such a night, he promised to buy you a remote controlled toy car, a motorbike-with-rider, a battery-powered train, a remote controlled toy plane, and a boat, among other things. You might actually make him feel guilty enough to buy you the one thing you really wanted, which was a motorbike-with-rider.

The meal over, the younger children were excused and they scampered away with unusual speed. The adults looked at their disappearing backs longingly as Mr. Napoleon Lebulu carried on and on about political fish getting themselves cooked in their own oil; and how losing your culture is slavery and we must stick to our culture no matter what and, many other original ideas of that type.

Regarding the one about sticking to your culture no matter what, Aoro dared interject,

"I suppose the dinosaur thought exactly the same way before becoming extinct." Wandia and Alicia laughed. Johnny just continued looking at the fellow as if he couldn't believe his eyes. Leb went on as if Aoro had not spoken.

Finally Alicia, getting sick of it all, announced suddenly, "I think I will see you off, Leb." She stood up, cutting Leb off in mid sentence. He was having a great time trying to impress his possible future mother and father-in-law, and was about to protest when he caught the look in her eye. Quickly he stood up and said his effusive goodbyes.

The room was entirely silent when Alicia got back. All eyes asked the same question—*Why?*

"I want to marry him," she said, her voice sounding odd in the silent night. Then she left the room.

There was silence. Finally Wandia told the dazed Johnny,

"Call Sybil, I must talk to her. Something is not right here."

Johnny went to the phone and dialled Canada where it was still morning.

***

BRETT STANLEY CLUTCHED the slip of paper on which he had written the Sigu's address as if his life depended on it. And it surely did for hadn't he lived through sheer hell for almost a year? It was only a week ago that there had appeared a chink of light.

A few months back he had sent his sister Sybil a postcard from Zurich giving his address and telephone number— after six months of silence. *I just wanted you to know I'm Ok*, he wrote. She had sent one back with an equally bland message; *Everyone is well, please take care*. Nothing about the one person he longed to hear about.

Then one night his phone rang. He thought it was one of his students looking for help with a dissertation or something of that sort. But it was Sybil. She did not bother with any but the most rudimentary preliminaries.

"Listen, Brett, Alicia's in trouble. If I were you I

would take the next plane out of Zurich. I don't know why, but she imagines that she is in love with you. And I hear she is just about to marry the strangest fellow you ever heard of because she thinks you don't care about her."

"But that's not true!" he yelled.

"I can assure it is true. I spoke to her aunt less than an hour ago."

"I don't mean that! I mean it is not true that I don't care about her! I love her. I think of her constantly. I am going crazy just wanting to be with her!"

"For a professor of linguistics, you are very unclear sometimes. Anyway, get down to Nairobi as fast as you can." And she gave him the address and then hung up. Brett kept on swinging between seventh heaven and deepest hell as his imagination ran riot. Finally he extricated himself from his more urgent responsibilities and took a Swiss Air flight to Nairobi.

He instructed the taxi-man to wait and then knocked on the door of the largish house with uncharacteristic timidity. He had the great misfortune of having the door opened for him by none other than young Gandhi who had a ball under one arm and had obviously been on his way out to play.

"Hi!" said Gandhi.

"Hi!" answered Brett. The two regarded each other for a moment or two. Brett did not come up with anything else, and Gandhi was a busy fellow with many things to see to. He was about to slip out and leave

Brett marooned on the front step when the latter finally gathered his wits.

"My name is Brett Stanley. Does Alicia Courtney live here?"

"Are you her boyfriend too?" asked the inimitable Gandhi. Brett gulped and decided to take a plunge at the deep end.

"Yes." Gandhi looked him up and down with a judicial eye. Finally he said,

"I like you. You are much better than that funny man who came here to eat our food the other day." Then turning half way round he called out,

"Aliciaaa! Brett has come to see you!" Then he remembered that he had been told a dozen times not to yell out people's names, but rather to go and knock politely on their doors and tell them what needed to be told in a quiet voice. He decided to make his escape before someone came for his neck.

FIFTEEN

NEW LOVES, OLD HOPES

ALICIA AND BRETT announced that they wished to be married inside the month—to Aoro's horror and Wandia's relief. That Leb person had been rather a shock to the system, and as far as Wandia was concerned the sooner the girl married some normal human being the better.

"But we need time to organise the wedding!" Aoro lamented. "Besides, you have to give your father and step-mother time to get here."

"I'm sorry, uncle, but we don't want a show-case wedding. Brett and I have been talking with Father Tony and he has agreed to fit us in on a Wednesday afternoon, his least busy day. We want a very quiet wedding. Those family members who can come are of course welcome. We would like to eat a late lunch or early dinner at home with the more immediate family and then fly down to Mombasa so that the following day we can drive down to Watamu for our honeymoon. Apart from anything else Brett has to be back at work early next month."

"But people will feel so bad if you don't invite them, besides I thought that weddings were ever only performed on Saturdays! What is this about Tony fitting you in on a Wednesday? Is he out of his mind or something?" He looked to Wandia for help but it was clear that she was on Alicia's side. As far as she was concerned, people had turned the whole wedding thing into such a circus that the bride and groom were more than likely to begin married life not only exhausted, but broke—which could hardly be a recipe for a happy married life.

"I think I can understand what Alicia means. We won't keep it secret and I will prepare a wonderful dinner for any family member who wishes to come, but the simplicity of it all appeals to me." Aoro gave up. In any case the two were so obviously in love and Brett was such a nice guy—a vast improvement on Hitler or whatever his name was—who had even had the audacity to come to Aoro at his clinic to shamelessly plead his case.

"But she promised to marry me!" wailed Napoleon Lebulu practically grovelling at Aoro's feet, much to his receptionist's amusement. "*You* know that! And I am not poor. I will give you a good bride-price," *God! Where did that girl get this creep!*

"Do I look to you like a man eager for a bride-price? Let me tell you, sir, my family stopped selling women many generations ago!" Aoro spat out, feeling sorely tempted to sink his fist into the man's jaw.

"If you let her go with that *mzungu*, you will live to regret it bitterly," shouted Lebulu belligerently, but close to the door just in case he needed to make a rapid getaway. To avoid having to go to jail for manslaughter Aoro asked the security man to come conduct the man out the door.

So Brett and Alicia were married by Father Tony. The priest took quite a liking to Brett who had declared quite honestly that he was agnostic.

"But I love Alicia and this ceremony seems to mean a lot to her. I would do anything for her. But I really don't believe too much in this God thing, at least not as something out there. As far as I am concerned, I am it— what I make of my life is what matters."

"So you think that men are indeed gods, masters of their own destiny?" Fr. Tony asked with real interest, giving Brett his whole attention.

"Yeah, that's what I mean," Brett agreed, a bit defensively. After all this was not only the uncle of the girl he wanted to marry, but also that disquieting animal, a Roman Catholic priest.

"Did you know that Jesus of Nazareth thought the same thing? And look what they did to him! It is much safer to be an atheist and believe that man is just a rational animal and quite expendable, his death meaningless. So whether you make something of your life or not, what does it matter?" Brett had to agree to that kind of logic. Trouble was, he wanted to make something out of his life, especially now. His eyes dwelt speculatively on the woman sitting next to him.

"Do you intend to have children? She is a very beautiful girl."

Brett was quite taken aback by this sudden change of subject and the manner in which it had been asked—with such complete understanding, as if the man had been reading his mind.

But yes. Now that he had met the love of his life he wanted children. Of her. He wanted precisely to be the father of *her* children. He wanted to wrestle on the sitting room floor with her sons and bury his face in the sweet softness of her little girl's body. All born of his love for her. Yes, how he wanted children! But how could a celibate priest understand these things?

"Yes, I want children," he said defensively, once again.

"In a world like this? With nothing better to hope for? What a terrible responsibility to wilfully bring another human being into this cul-de-sac we call life!"

"I will protect them with my life. I will love them and give them a good life." Yet from the misty memory of a very distant past, he remembered another man who had loved his children and would have protected them with his life, yet had died and it was only the skinny but determined shoulders of a little girl that had done the herculean task of keeping the sky from caving in completely.

235

"Yes, man is like a god, but hardly in charge of his destiny. It becomes poignantly clear only when you look into the eyes of your child and see in them the profession of faith: *I believe in God the Father Almighty, for is he not my Daddy who loves me and who will keep me safe always?* It must be hard having another human being totally dependent on you and not look elsewhere for hope and perhaps even courage."

Brett's swift and intelligent mind went a step further, *what, in fact, would I do if anything happened to this child of our love—if my protectiveness fell short and though alive I was unable to protect him from disease or accident and he therefore became maimed or even died?* He shook his head slowly from side to side as if to clear it.

"Why," Father Tony asked, changing the subject once again, "do two people commit themselves to such an adventurous and intrinsically impossible undertaking as marriage?"

"I love her. With love it is not impossible."

"You say you are in love, by which I suppose you mean that when you look into each other's eyes, your heart rate doubles, your palm becomes sweaty and your breathing shallower. However, after a few years you will become so familiar that if there is an increase in your heart rate it will probably be because of fury, not romantic inclination."

Brett and Alicia laughed in total disbelief at the very idea that they could ever look at each other with indifference or even with anger.

"It will happen. When it does, remember that marriage is a fusion of two people and that love is not necessarily something you feel despite all the romantic literature around. There are some things which are transcendental. Marriage is one of them; and that is why human beings attempt it again and again, despite all odds." And with that, together with the time he had spent talking to them, he felt confident enough to pronounce them husband and wife.

In spite of the short notice and purely informal word of mouth publicity there were at least one hundred friends and relatives who had abandoned their work to come to the wedding.

The mob also invited itself to the Sigu house afterwards and emergency rations had to be found for them all. But the truth of the matter is that if you give any Kenyan a leg to roast and something with which to chase it down, he would most certainly feel that he had been fed extraordinarily well. And as it turned out, Odongo Sigu, the farmer, had fortunately had the foresight to bring several such legs with him, to say nothing of ribs and *matumbo* (entrails). Several other people brought the requisite libation and in no time at all, the party was on its way. No way was such a daughter going to get married without a celebration, rationalised those who cared to rationalise. Hadn't marriage always been a community affair? When else could the elders legitimately get together? It didn't seem to matter much that most of these self-proclaimed elders were black-haired graduates with several degrees.

Brett looked askance at this impromptu gathering of humanity.

"I thought we wanted a quiet wedding?" he asked as the fiftieth unknown hand pumped his own hand enthusiastically.

"Yes," Alicia answered unperturbed. She knew that Africans consider almost anything a cause for celebration. "But three weeks is long enough for word to have gone round that I was getting married. They would feel that they had not done their duty if they had not personally come to wish me a happiness. The extended family came to my rescue when my mother died; and now they have come to share my happiness. It is only natural, and besides they mean no harm."

"Of course not," Brett had to agree. Alicia was sad because John and Sybil couldn't come. Sybil was meant to go to hospital on this very day for delivery by Caesarean section.

"And guess what! They are twins!" an excited Andrea had yelled so loudly as to make several thousand miles sound like just across the room. Alicia had had to move the phone several inches from her ear to prevent permanent damage to her ear drum.

There was a long distance scuffle as Sybil grabbed the phone from her daughter.

"Alicia! Are you still there? Honestly this child is fit for the asylum! Why did I imagine that I needed another one? But believe me she is *so* excited, she's called all our friends to tell them the *good* news. Of course, many of them are concerned about my sanity. *Aren't you too old dear?* You'd think I'm a doddering old granny. But we are both so sorry not to be there with you. John is completely torn, but I guess he has no choice but to be here with me especially as I will require so much assistance. I love you and I am confident that both of you will be happy. Brett is a lucky man. Tell him to watch his step—or else!" Sybil had hung up laughing.

Too soon it was five o'clock and the two newly-weds had to rush down to the airport for their trip down to the coastal town of Mombasa.

Aoro and Wandia stood side by side waving to them as they disappeared through the door marked *Departures*.

Wandia had such a peculiar look on her face that Aoro felt compelled to ask whether she was alright.

She shook her head, and then shook it again.

"The first one is gone. I just had a strong premonition of the swift emptying of the nest. Sooner than we realise young Mark will be disappearing through a gate marked 'departures' too." She had a sense that time, always swift in its passage, had picked up momentum and was hurtling along and with it, all destiny.

"Yes, my love, but before Alicia, Mark, and all the others there was just you and I. And I think someone has asked this question before ever I did, but let me repeat it: 'Am I not more to you than ten sons?'"

"Of course you are more to me than any number of sons." But in her woman's heart she thought, *I have carried children under my heart. It is not something one can explain.*

The evening had been made more peculiar by the fact that the hitherto happy-go-lucky Johnny had turned up with a girl to whom he seemed to pay extraordinary attention. She was a rather tall and confident looking young woman, definitely not Johnny's usual type of hysterical female. There was, however, something disquietingly familiar about her, so familiar that Aoro had finally asked;

"Haven't I met you somewhere before?"

"Not that I can remember," the girl answered with a smile that only made Aoro more convinced that he was right.

"You will forgive my forgetfulness please, but what did you say your last name was?"

"I didn't," she answered glancing at Johnny who was fussing around her like a mother hen with an only chick.

"Ah I forgot to introduce her properly," he said bobbing up and down like a teenager on his first date, "This is Kandake Muhambe. Kandi, my uncle, Dr. Aoro Sigu."

Aoro's mouth fell open for a moment.

"Your father is not a Thomas Muhambe by any chance?"

"You know my dad?" The girl started laughing at

the odd look on Aoro's face and then stopped unsure of the situation. But her father was such an excellent man and she loved him so much that she could not imagine that anyone who knew him would harbour anything but admiration and respect.

"My God! You are brave old Tommy's daughter! Your father and I grew up in the same neighbourhood in Nakuru; in fact," and here he faltered a little, "he was a close family friend of ours."

"Oh!" was all the young lady could think to say. Johnny looked gratified. Aoro on his part went off abruptly to look for Wandia. When he found her he dragged her aside and told her;

"I never told you this, but before Vera's vocation she had a friend—a very good friend. And believe it or not, Johnny has turned up with the man's daughter and for once he looks serious."

He pointed the girl out and as fate would have it she looked up just at that instant. So Aoro did the only decent thing he could do—he took the surprised Wandia over to be introduced.

Both had more or less the same thought on their minds. *This could have been Vera's daughter.*

And Kandake, whose name was the corrected and African version of *Candace* the Queen of Sheba, became instantaneously beloved of the Sigu household without knowing why everyone treated her like a long lost daughter. It didn't help that when she took Johnny home to meet her parents, her father's expression was even more shaken than Aoro's when she explained who Johnny's guardian was.

***

WHEN ONE IS in a glass-bottomed boat at Watamu, one has to make certain clear-cut decisions—either to pay attention to your brand-new husband or to the explosion of colour and movement at the bottom of the sea. Alicia weighed the question and decided that a husband is always with one, but that she may never see Watamu again. So she gave herself to gasps and shrieks of incredulous delight as strange fish, which rivalled the rainbow itself in iridescent colour, darted here and there among the delicately sculptured fronds of coral which grew in the undersea gardens of delight.

Brett, on the other hand, was in a pensive mood. He kept on thinking about the things that Father Tony Sigu had said, or rather the things he had left unsaid. They made him feel vaguely disturbed as if someone had shifted the furniture around in a room which had been previously taken for granted due to its familiar comfort. The uncertain certitudes upon which he had constructed his life's philosophy had skid a little from under him and he could not determine why. After all he was an intelligent and well-educated person, surely he could never subscribe to the limitations of any organised religion as an explanation for existence?

He wished Alicia would look up and talk to him. Or just look at him with those eyes which could banish all the vague misgivings which had chosen his honeymoon, of all occasions, to plague his mind. But as of this moment in time, he had lost her to the angelfish, the porcupine fish and the moonfish. Why would fish which live in the depths of the sea feel so strong a need to bedeck themselves in such gay colours anyway? Brett was beginning to get jealous. Suddenly she sat up and looking straight at him smiled with such brilliant joy that his heart lurched.

And in that smile, Brett Stanley found new moorings for his life and the direction he must take in these first halting years of a new Millennium.

He sought her hand and held it.

Sixteen

A MAN AND HIS QUEEN

DR JOHN SIGU COURTNEY, gloved and gowned, stood with his hands clasped together as if in prayer. In front of him lay the patient shrouded to the neck. The only part which had been left exposed was the abdomen—scrubbed and ready to be sliced open. The nature of the surgery was listed as an 'exploratory laparotomy' which in normal language simply meant 'cut and see'. The man had had left loin pain for about a month, but investigations had been inconclusive though they pointed more or less at a collection of pus in the *psoas* muscle. The only worrisome thing was that the man had noticed blood in his urine. The *psoas* was one of the powerful muscles which anchored the back of the abdomen to the pelvis.

At the patient's head, the anaesthetist, Dr Kiptarus Yegon worked to ensure that the vital signs of life were well maintained and that the patient was well anaesthetised—that is totally free from pain, as well as completely relaxed—so that the surgeon could cut through the muscles. This total immobilisation of muscles of course rendered the patient unable to breath for himself and therefore he was connected to a respirator which expanded his lungs mechanically and periodically filled them with a mixture of oxygen and anaesthetic gasses. It required skill and calm to maintain the patient in this kind of artificially-induced coma without letting him sink too deep or come too close to the surface. Dr Yegon had heard of cases of patients who, though immobilised, remained conscious and could therefore hear the doctors and nurses complaining about their salaries and horrible working conditions!

As far as operations went this was a pretty routine one, but for Dr. Courtney it was a very special one for this was the very first time he was standing on the right side of the patient and operating as the 'senior surgeon'. His consultant, to show his determination not to participate and his confidence in Courtney, was lounging around outside in the corridors—unscrubbed and ungowned, but within calling distance.

Johnny steadied his heart and reminded himself that he had watched this operation and others similar to it being done, had assisted in them and had himself done it at least once—but with his consultant assisting. And that there always had to be a first time. And that it was an honour—as far as he knew, none of the other residents in surgery had gone solo yet.

"We are ready," announced Dr Yegon into the expectant air.

"Scalpel!' demanded the surgeon, no longer just himself but part of a combat-ready team, trained to fight death at death's own terms.

Before the words were out of his mouth, Theatre Nurse Wamalwa slapped the instrument into his open palm. And the operation was on its way.

Dr Courtney worked his way into the abdominal cavity and moved the coils of intestine out of his way to give him a view of the psoas, but half way there he found something that made him inhale sharply. It was an ominous-looking fungating growth whose center had liquefied giving it the appearance of an abscess, but in actual fact the collection of fluid consisted of dead and dying tissue. To the young surgeon, the whole thing looked suspiciously like cancer. But from where? The patient was forty-seven and apart from the moderate pain, had appeared well and had been at work up to the day before his admission.

"Call Dr Matagaro please."

As the consultant scrubbed and gowned himself, Dr Courtney did a thorough exploration of the abdominal cavity to see whether he could pick up any more clues regarding the possible source of the growth. The only thing he could see were the markedly enlarged lymph nodes around the aorta. He reported his findings

o Dr Matagaro who suggested that the best thing was
o excise some of the growth and the nodes and then
o close the abdomen and await pathology reports. The
rowth looked truly ugly perhaps a rhabdomyosarcoma
—a nasty aggressive tumour of muscle, usually
mpossible to treat. A death sentence really.

Dr Courtney passed his fingers around the mass
gain. Despite its ugly appearance the tumour seemed
o have a pretty clear margin. A strong feeling came
ver Johnny. It was almost an aura—powerful and
lmost tangible. This was the first time he had
xperienced it but little did he know that it would come
o him many times in his life thereafter—and always
hen faced with a tricky medical situation in which
omebody's hold on life was hanging by a mere whisker.

The essence of the feeling was that all that stood
etween the utter sadness of the cessation, the beauty
nd grace of living were the skills bequeathed to him
hrough many years of study and apprenticeship. He
ould not give up, or rather could not give up! *I Swear
y all that I hold sacred and dear*, he prayed silently
nd then said aloud:

"Sir, I think we should at least attempt a complete
esection." His voice was a little thick with the power
f his feeling and determination.

Dr Matagaro studied his student's face—the steady
yes, still hands and set jaw. The training in medicine,
specially at specialist level, is ultimately one of instilling
willingness to accept responsibility, creating an ability

to execute judgment and carry out therapy and finall
an acceptance of the bleak knowledge that the buc
could not be passed further up to any one else. D
Matagaro realised that Dr Courtney had come a
medical age. He therefore nodded his head slightly an
walked out—clearly leaving Johnny to take the full weigl
of his decision.

Johnny did an extensive resection of growth. H
was meticulous and thorough, but towards the end a
the operation, just as he was about to start closing th
layers of the abdomen, the patient who had been quit
stable up to this point, suddenly went into a cardia
arrest. Just like that. The alarm went off and Johnn
stared at the cardiac monitor in disbelief. Instead a
the normal regularly spaced spikes that would have bee
there, the line was flat with only an occassional blip.

With Dr Yegon taking control of the situation th
entire team swung into a well rehearsed drill to resta
the stalled heart. It was at such moments that on
appreciated the presence of a calm, intelligen
anaesthetist. Someone started to massage the heart—
procedure which, despite its name, looked more lik
trying to break the patient's ribs. The electri
defillibrator was brought and its leads placed on th
patient's chest. Dr Yegon flicked a switch and a surg
of electricity passed through the patient, causing hin
to arch up from the operating table. Shocked at th
rude treatment, the heart started to beat again, thoug
reluctantly. Dr Yegon pumped in several potent drug

and the heart steadied sufficiently for the operation to be completed.

Dr Courtney then closed the abdomen and the anaesthetist began the process of reversing the patient from anaesthetic coma. This was surprisingly uneventful and the patient was soon telling the story of his life in a grumpy confused voice. Just to be on the safe side they sent him to ICU for observation. It turned out that he had a rare congenital disorder of the pumping action of the heart which had only shown up due to the stress of surgery and low oxygen tension characteristic of surgery.

In half an hour Dr Courtney was scrubbed and gowned again, ready to start on his second patient of the day.

Six hours and three patients later, Johnny stepped into the changing-rooms, peeled off his theatre clothing, and resumed his out-of-theatre personality again. As he did so he whistled softly under his breath—a sound filled with a sense of personal satisfaction. Feeling that this was not enough, he did a quick war dance. This made him burst into self-deprecating laughter.

"You OK, Courtney?" came a concerned voice from the next changing room.

"OK? That must be the understatement of the year—I feel great!"

He stepped in front of the mirror to neaten up his tie and then, opening the two doors which separated the theatre world from the rest of the world, he stepped out. He needed to make an urgent call.

Johnny had every reason to feel great indeed. Three months ago he had received his pilot's licence. Soon he would qualify as a general surgeon. And finally he had a standing offer to join a team of flying doctors on a part time basis. He would spend the rest of the time working at the teaching hospital. What more could a man want surely? One little thing. Only one little thing! And he wanted to see her tonight!

Some of the elation left him as he thought of her. Why wouldn't she commit herself to him after all the time they had known each other? It was so ego-denting to love a woman who thought so little of you. Johnny had a pretty good inkling as to why Kandake seemed intent to treat him as a rather distant friend and their relationship as purely platonic. Maybe she was interested in someone else. The mere thought made Johnny's stomach churn with jealousy. But no: Kandi was not the kind of young woman to keep a man dangling.

She had, however, advised him more than once to look for a different kind of woman because she herself felt that she could ever only live with a man she could fully trust—not some God-forsaken playboy.

It was pointless to point out to her that since the day he had met her he had never looked at any other woman unless it was for the purpose of operating on her. The whole issue had to be resolved soon. After all he was approaching thirty-two and she was twenty-eight, they were hardly that young any more. He had met her at a graduation party that he had organised with some of his friends when he was still a hilarious youth of twenty-six and filled with conviction that he was not only a clever fellow, but a pretty wonderful one and any woman should be grateful to be noticed by him. But not Kandi, he soon discovered to his amazement. He therefore pursued her relentlessly.

At first she had just wanted to complete her degree in Diplomatic Studies. Thereafter she joined the Ministry of Foreign Affairs and she was just beginning to thaw out when a group of his former girlfriends planned a coup that almost destroyed the relationship.

Johnny was sitting at the bar of the little restaurant he and Kandi had made into a regular meeting place waiting for her to join him when one of his former girlfriends appeared looking as innocent as little baby Jesus on Christmas Day. Johnny didn't know that two others were positioned outside as look-outs.

"Hi Johnny! *Umepotea!* One hardly sees you any more these days. How are you doing?"

"I'm fine Sylvie. How are you?" He regarded her with mild interest. She was a very pretty girl with a full voluptuous figure which he had once found very attractive.

"Buy an old friend a drink, will you?" she pouted prettily at him.

He started shaking his head,

"I'm waiting for..." She cut him short.

"You young doctors are always broke. *I'll* buy you a drink. *Barman!*"

The next few seconds were a nightmare in slow motion. Before the barman could react, another of Johnny's old flames stepped into the restaurant and nodded lightly in their direction. Not realising that it was a signal, Johnny nodded back, grinning a little foolishly. Before he knew what was happening to him Sylvie was all over him, her lips glued to his like a blood-sucking leech to its victim. Johnny tried to disentangle himself from her and in the confusion, he saw Kandi walking into the room looking like sunshine on a cold day. The look on her face changed rapidly from one of joyous anticipation to disbelief and finally to utter betrayal. Kandi stumbled out just as Johnny finally succeeded in dragging Sylvie off him with such force that the momentum threw her halfway across the room into a confused pile of human, table and chair legs, to say nothing of cutlery and crockery. But Kandi never saw it.

Johnny did not so much as pause to find out whether Sylvie was dead or alive. He bounded after Kandi only to see her back disappearing into a taxi.

Then began six months of agony. She would neither see him nor talk to him, nor allow him anywhere near her.

"Serves you right," Wandia told him when she heard the story and Johnny's protestations of absolute innocence. "You used to enjoy having all those girls swarming all over you, no discrimination at all. Just a little fun—remember? They meant nothing to you. But people have hearts and they get hurt. You finally meet

Kandi and you dump all these girls as if they never existed. In your arrogance you expect them to understand and walk away meekly. If I was Kandi I would have thrown a glass at you before walking away for ever. You don't deserve her."

"But auntie! It's all so unfair. There was never anything between me and these girls, I swear! They were just friends!"

"Friends don't do the kind of things they did to you. Grow up for heavens' sake."

***

WHILE JOHNNY'S CAREER flourished, his love life foundered. But Kandi, in spite of herself, loved Johnny and Johnny loved Kandi to the point of distraction—especially now that it looked like she would never become his. Slowly they got together again, but though Johnny popped the vital question almost every day, Kandi was too afraid to commit herself to a man who seemed to draw women to him like a magnet. So she kept on saying no and with heart in mouth, urged him to look for someone with that kind of suicidal courage.

Meanwhile just to make things more complicated, Kandi had just been appointed an attache to Kenya's ambassador to Korea. And since the relationship with Johnny appeared to be going nowhere, Kandi did not see any reason to resist the move which would take her half way round the world from him.

Johnny was desperate and Kandi totally worn-out.

***

"Come in 5 Yankee Delta Foxtrot Alpha. Do you read me?"

"Reading you loud and clear. What's up?"

"Balloon smash-up in the Mara, near the Sarova Lodge. Five people injured, three seriously. You are nearest the scene. Please reroute your plane. Repeat reroute your plane."

Johnny had had no difficulty finding a part time job with Eastern Africa Medical Airlift as a flying doctor. He was in the truly enviable position of being a surgeon who could fly and he had had several offers. He was, however, keen on keeping up regular hospital practice and so could only accept a part-time job.

Today, with fellow pilot Greg Flynn and Flight Nurse Ilana Mwandawiro, he had been to pick up a Maasai youth who had been badly mauled by a lion while herding cattle. The youth had fought the lion ferociously eventually killing it, but he was terribly torn up. The lion had laid open the youth's abdomen with one final swipe of its dying paw and Johnny found him with half his gut spilling out. He had other ghastly wounds but Johnny was most worried about this one. What was surprising was that he was conscious and could talk, though with difficulty.

"How are you?" Johnny asked to distract the youth as he rapidly worked on him, patching up what could be patched up and putting pressure dressings on the rest. He really didn't expect an answer. Flight Nurse

Mwandawiro expertly inserted a large bore cannula into a vein on the boy's muscular arm and started to infuse plasma expanders at a rapid rate.

"Hapana mbaya sana, daktari," the gallant youth whispered —which meant 'not too bad, doctor'.

Now if there was anything Johnny admired in a human being, it was courage. He hoped the boy would make it. It was not for nothing the Maasai had been called the Romans of Eastern Africa.

"What is his name,?" he asked the clan members who had accompanied the youth.

"Kantai ole Saisi," answered an elderly man. "He is my son."

"I have to take him with me. He is very badly wounded and there is very little I can do here. You have to sign a form giving me permission to operate when I get him to hospital." Flight Nurse Mwandawiro produced a form and an ink-pad for a thumb print, but old Kantai had gone to a mission school long ago as a boy and waving away the ink-pad, he took a biro and printed his name proudly on the indicated spot.

"Take care of him. He is a good boy and is doing very well at school. He is also very brave, as you can see, and in spite of his great learning helps us look after the cattle during the school holidays."

The boy was in third-form at a local secondary school and was obviously the apple of his father's eye. But nobody shed a tear or wailed. The Maasai personality is stoic.

They put the youth in the plane, strapped him onto a stretcher and were airborne when the instructions came for the plane to reroute to the Maasai Mara which probably meant a delay of up to an hour or more.

"How are the vital signs ?" He asked the nurse.

"Respirations 40. Pulse 100. Blood pressure 95 over 60 and coming up. I don't think he is haemorrhaging any more, doctor."

"Come in control, come in control. Do you read me?"

"This is control. We read you loud and clear. Proceed."

"Our patient is stable. We are rerouting to the Mara. Over."

"Thank you doc. Over and out."

As Captain Flynn flew the Cessna over the expansive Loita plains, Johnny remembered a particularly hair-raising experience he had had while flying north over Samburu in another rescue mission. Two of the Samburu cattle wandered right onto the runway just as Johnny was about to touch down. He hit a cow instead, but had the presence of mind to get airborne again so fast that the other occupants had no idea what had actually happened to make the plane lurch so wildly. They had had to abandon mission and send in another plane late in the afternoon. The day ended with an emergency landing at Wilson airport.

Now at the Mara something had gone wrong with the mechanism of the balloon and it had crashed into the side of a hill. Two of the occupants were badly injured with multiple fractures of various limbs. One man had sustained severe head injuries and was comatose. The others had escaped with comparatively minor injuries.

Dr Courtney and Flight Nurse Mwandawiro worked furiously—putting up drips and arresting bleeding. Johnny inserted a tube down the wind pipe of the comatose man so that his already laboured respirations could be assisted artificially. If they had been better prepared there would at least have been an extra Flight Nurse, but as it was they had to make do. Johnny was grateful that Ilana Mwandawiro was a particularly competent nurse and well trained in resuscitation techniques.

Soon they were airborne again, this time with Captain Flynn at the controls of the Fokker 10. Johnny knew that soon they would be in Nairobi with helpful hands waiting to receive the patients, but for the time being his hands were full. Captain Flynn flew the plane carefully, avoiding obvious turbulence areas. He was especially concerned about the man with the head injuries—Johnny had told him that he suspected damage to the spine as well, which meant that a bad jolt could paralyse the man completely.

The plane approached Wilson Airport from the direction of the Nairobi Game Park and flying low over the houses that some thoughtless idiot had allowed to be built there, Flynn landed the Fokker 10 as if the runway was made of eggshells. In a minute the plane was surrounded by all kinds of nurses and paramedics and Johnny could finally allow himself the luxury of feeling tired.

To his delighted and disbelieving amazement, Kandi was there to meet him. It had never happened before. Johnny snapped out a few orders and dashed through his report. Soon he and Kandi were flying down Langata Road in her new girl-sized Polo. Johnny's heart leapt into his mouth. Maybe she wanted to kill both of them and be done with it once and for all.

"Would you slow down a bit," he suggested as mildly as he could as she narrowly missed a swinging petrol-tanker trailer by a whisker while overtaking a Mercedes. A Mercedes for heaven's sake!

"Are you angry with me?" he ventured. "I mean, angrier than usual?"

"No, but I wonder how long it takes a man who is intelligent enough to be a flying surgeon to propose, especially when the long-suffering girl has been waiting patiently for over five years?"

"Are you asking me to marry you?" Johnny asked too surprised to think up a more romantic way of phrasing his question.

"No, I'm telling you it's high time you asked me to marry you!"

"Kandi, will you marry me?" he asked quickly before he could wake up from the dream.

"Yes, Johnny." He felt like making her swear it on the Bible but he didn't have one, and maybe she would not have taken kindly to the idea. Some girl.

"But why? I mean what happened?"

"Is this a court-martial or something? Does a girl have to answer all these questions when someone asks her to marry him?"

"You know very well what I mean! I've been asking every day for years! What have I suddenly done right?"

"Well, if you must know, two of your old girlfriends finally became conscience-stricken and came to tell me the whole story, plus a few other things which made me feel that there might still be hope for you—does that make you happy?"

"Very much. Could you stop the car so that I could demonstrate it?"

"No Johnny, nobody stops on Langata Road unless they want to become a widow even before they are married. I really must live long enough to marry you—else all the waiting would have been in vain."

***

JOHNNY'S AND KANDAKE'S wedding was very colourful if only because of the amazing crew who were invited or who invited themselves. The best man was Andrew Karama, architect, who had cheated death so many times that it had become something of a joke between himself and his best friend Johnny. Andy had not only managed to qualify, but was a much sought-after architect for the sheer wizardry he brought to the art of building. He was often sick, but when he was well he worked with the energy of a man who knew the preciousness of each passing minute. Andy brought quite a few friends from the Society of People with Aids and they were just ordinary men and women fighting a terrible disease while trying to live as normally as possible. Nice guys some of whom had wives or husbands, and children—young children because many of the infected were so painfully young.

In the back, spear in hand and in the full regalia of a young warrior stood Kantai ole Saisi— his red toga-like *shuka* blowing in the gentle wind. He almost stole the show and would have, had the bride not been so radiant. She had chosen to be married in a gold-tinted African dress with a brilliantly done up headdress from which fell a little veil. The entire ensemble made her look regal—the best of Africa. Between Andy and Kantai were the rest of humanity. Every one was in a festive mood. Fr. Tony was in attendance.

"I can see that you and your sister have diametrically opposed views in your concepts of what a fitting nuptial should be," he said to the groom smiling.

"Listen, uncle. I've worked damned hard to get this girl and I've waited too long for this day. I want the whole bloody world to know—that yes, *that girl there is mine!*"

"OK, OK!" said the priest his hands lifted in mock surrender. "In that case I too shall look for vestments to fit the occasion. You and your sister make me feel that after all, my poor sister Rebecca's sad life has been somewhat vindicated!"

But Johnny had decided to let that old demon rest. He wanted to be happy. He *was* happy.

This time John and Sybil were there. Andrea had been left in charge of her twin brothers who, according to their mother, would have been fitting inmates for the local zoo—but the zookeeper had apparently declined on the grounds that they would be a bad influence on the animals. A self-assured young lady, Andrea had however called her step-brother to wish him every happiness.

Alicia and Brett came with their two-year-old daughter—Wandia. Quite overcome, the older Wandia shed tears of joy when they placed the child in her arms.

Johnny's colleagues from the Eastern Africa Medical Airlift were there in their starched navy blue and white uniforms. There was also a whole crowd of former classmates.

Thomas Muhambe gave his daughter away. He was seen craning his neck around in an interesting fashion and people wondered whether he had a stiff neck or something, but no— he was trying to get a glimpse of his old flame Vera, but Vera had been unable to come. To send Kandi off were all kinds of people from the diplomatic world —suave and urbane men and women who knew how to move around without causing tremors.

In the midst of this glittering gathering of men and women, John Sigu Courtney took Kandake Muhambe to be the queen of his heart.

Sixteen

AWAY TO THE MARA

JOHNNY, WHO HAD FLOWN the length and breadth of most of Eastern Africa, and who therefore knew its greatest beauty spots decided to take his bride to the Maasai Mara for their honeymoon.

"We will drive down the old Naivasha way—the way it hugs the side of the escarpment as it descends to the floor of the Rift Valley makes for a very impressive view. We will then branch off for Narok when we are near Hells Gate park by Mt. Longonot." Kandi looked at Johnny and smiled.

"From Narok we will drive across the Loita plains— that should provide some interesting sights. I think we should reach the Simba Safari Lodge at the Mara in time for lunch. The Mara in Kenya, and the Serengeti in Tanzania together form, in sheer vastness, beauty, plenitude and variety of animal and birdlife, a visual and spiritual feast. I know you will love it."

She nodded not really listening, but finding the sound of his voice a joy.

"Sounds OK." She really didn't mind, just being away and with him was wonderful enough.

Johnny drove through the lush green countryside his eyes taking in the peaceful sight of farmers going about their business. Little barefoot boys taking a little time off from helping their parents, were playing by the roadside. The African child must make his weight felt from a very early age. Some might consider it child labour, apparently believing that a child had the right to play unhampered, with only occasional breaks to go to school and hopefully learn something, without too much stress, of course. However, he knew that these children were learning valuable skills from their parents—among them order and organisation—which would stand them in excellent stead at school and in later life. Once a friend of his had described what his day had been like as a boy in the village on his family's plot of land,

"I would wake up at five in the morning to milk our two or three dairy cows because the milk had to be by the road at six-thirty ready for collection. I would then rush back to wash my face in cold water, get dressed, gulp down a cup of *uji* and run to school almost three miles away—there was simply no question of walking or I would have been late and my teacher would never have countenanced that. That chap was tough, I tell you! The result was that by the time I got to class I was so charged with adrenaline that had the teacher started teaching in Greek or Chinese I would have understood him. In the evening I reversed the order for I had chores to do at home and homework to complete with a hurricane lamp. I was among the lucky; many children had to do the same with a tin lamp. One of these is currently a lecturer in engineering at the University of Nairobi. The truth is, having it tough can often give a fellow a boost in very unexpected ways, so much so that I think my own children who have everything and attend expensive schools are seriously deprived, not to say dangerously handicapped. I tell you, by the time I was ten I was in charge of my destiny. My son is in charge of nothing that I know of, though his need for unearned money is insatiable."

The man, a brilliant lawyer, had also pointed out that many of the village children had to work for money to pay their way through school or else the family finances would not have allowed it. Every Saturday they would be out picking pyrethrum, tea, coffee or doing whatever job was available. A child was a valuable and resourceful person within his family and thus had not been regarded as a burden until very recent times. Rarely did the child feel put upon or exploited, he was contributing—as was every member of his family. The lawyer had also felt that keeping a child dependent on his parents or the state for long periods of time was, in a way, encouraging a very dangerous form of parasitism. Pretty soon a whole crowd of people began to think that the world owed them an easy life.

"When this easy life cannot be provided they turn nasty. From the age of fifteen they should spend two weeks of every school holiday working on farms, public works and factories as part of learning about the world of work, with their hands actually on the job. From this they should earn pocket money and part of their school fees, to say nothing about earning extra marks for things like industriousness and order." The man had sent his protesting son to one of his farms and Johnny had thought that rather drastic, but the man had been deadly serious. Being a lawyer, he probably had a clearer idea about the genesis of crime than had most people. It did seem wasteful to keep hordes of young people constantly chained to books, and, what was worse, make them believe that this was a gateway to a nice (read not too demanding but very well paying) job.

Johnny rounded the bend and came across two noisy boys on a donkey-cart laden with farm produce of some kind or other. He slowed down and noticed that the bigger one was wielding a wicked looking stick and that the donkey was not too well looked after. He stopped and regarded the boy and the beast.

"*Jambo kijana,*" he greeted him.

"*Jambo bwana,*" the boy answered politely thinking that it was some city slicker who had lost his way and was in need of direction.

"That's a nice donkey you have there. I am a doctor you know, though I treat different kinds of animals, and I was thinking that if you fed such a nice donkey well, he would be strong enough to pull the cart without you having to beat him so much." He drove off as the boy's mouth fell open. City slickers rarely ever stopped to bother with anyone let alone talk to them. Johnny saw him waving as he rounded another corner. Kandi laughed.

He breathed in the good, bracing, country air, free of the fumes and effluvia of modern living, and felt elated and alive in every fibre of his being. Johnny glanced at the woman beside him and held his breath afraid that maybe he was dreaming again. Then he reached out for her hand just to assure himself that he was awake and not in the grip of some rather pleasant dream.

Soon they began the dramatic descent down the shoulder of the escarpment of the Great Rift Valley. The road twisted this way and that, searching for a foothold on the steep mountainside. Dozens of rolling hills and small mountains hugged the floor of the Great Rift looking like a whole lot of beached prehistoric monsters, caught unawares by the ebbing tide of time.

Away to the left he soon caught sight of Mt Longonot looking like a tired dinosaur with its head down with its ridges of cooled lava resembling gaunt ribs, and a great tail stretching out behind. The vegetation had changed from lush highland tropical to endless plains of savanna grasslands the colour of old gold flecked with rusty green—a paradise for a fair proportion of the animals of the world. He could already see some of them, frolicking impalas and fat bottomed zebras which surely must have been created on a day when God was feeling even more hilarious than usual. But he was driving too fast to stop and look—he still had a long drive ahead of him and he knew that the last section of the road was a true back breaker and in any case they would see thousands of animals once at the Maasai Mara National Reserve.

At the Ewaso Nyiro river Kandi, who had dozed off, started up and looked listlessly at the passing plains. However she soon took interest when they started passing herds upon herds of animals.

"Look, look!" she said in childlike delight.

"I'd love to honey, but I'm afraid I can't. I happen to be driving." She giggled at that. *What a lovely sound,* she thought.

At the Sekenani Gate, Johnny went to present their papers to the game rangers while a crowd of colourfully dressed Maasai women crowded around the car to sell her their magnificent bead-work. She bought a choker from a pearly-toothed woman who spoke impressive tourist pidgin;

"No problem, madam, no problem," she declared. "Five hundred shillings only!"

"But that's too expensive! I'm not a tourist, I'm a citizen—*mimi ni mwananchi!* Two hundred shillings only."

"No problem, no problem. Three hundred!" And

Kandake realised that her entire repertoire of English consisted of those two words plus a good grasp of numbers. Swahili was not a necessity this far away from the hustle and bustle of town life. She parted company with the money and got the bright coloured necklace. It would be a great accessory for her African dress.

Johnny got back behind the wheel and soon they were at the Mara Simba Lodge which was built right on the bank of the River Talek which, along with the Olare Orok, the Nitakitiak, the Olkeju Rongai, and the Sand River flowed into the great Mara River. From time immemorial, a paradise must have rivers and these were the rivers of the paradise of Mara.

They were just in time to be shown their room, freshen up a bit and then appear for a much-needed and excellent lunch. A crocodile day-dreamed at the bank of the river below, no doubt praying that an earthquake would suddenly topple the great logs upon which the open dining area was built, sending every one down to the river where he lay waiting. However as no such thing happened, he waded away to look for some more honestly earned lunch.

After lunch they rested for a couple of hours and then went for a guided evening game drive. There had been unseasonally heavy rains and the place was like a meadow—awash with waves upon waves of tall grass, dotted with clumps of dark green shrubs, thorny black and yellow-boled acacias and dozens of *Euphorbia Candelabra* whose many arms were raised up to the sun in worship.

There were endless herds of animals. Grazers pulled up tufts of grass, while browsers curled their agile tongues around the leaves of the clumps of shrubs the most conspicuous of which was the aromatic *Leleshua* some of whose leaves were a surprising bright orange in an otherwise green background.

The guide counted so many types of gazelles and antelopes that Kandi gave up trying to keep up. There were impalas, Grants gazelles and Thomsons gazelles. There were kongonis, klipspringers, steinboks and Topis. There were little dik-diks and jumpy duikers. There were also comically ugly gnus which were purportedly so brainless that they hurled themselves to a heedless death when the passion for migration overtook them—anything rather than remain behind. Vying with the gnus for sheer ugliness were the warthogs, but unlike the lugubrious gnus, the warthogs had arrogant overconfident personalities, strutting around with swinging bottoms, tails pointing straight into the air like victory flags.

In the following days they saw two elephants, the proud and protective parents of a young jumbo. There was a lioness and her cubs and they also spotted a cheetah feeding under the shade of some scrubs. A giraffe, unbelievably graceful and beautiful looked soulfully at her mate. A crook-gaited hyena trotted along with impressive purposefulness

"The giraffe is the only animal incapable of making any sound whatsoever," intoned the all-knowing guide.

"What! No sounds at all? Even when dying?" Kandi could not believe that soundlessness could exist naturally in so advanced an animal. It seemed like a terrible deprivation—to be unable to utter a sound—of pain, of sorrow, of joy, of protest. But latter she read in her guide book that the giraffe can and does make a sound, but only under extreme duress, for example if an infant is being attacked or is killed by predators. A mother to the core of its gentle soul is the giraffe.

The birdlife at the Mara was also quite impressive. Both Kandi and Johnny were completely taken up by the shimmery blues, reds, greens and yellows that the eye encountered at every turn. The secretary bird, 'quill pens' stuck around its head, stalked its prey, including snakes, among the tall savanna grasses. A pair of crested cranes, obviously aware of their beauty, posed for photographs like professional models. As if several gleaming colours were not enough, they also had a golden halo-like crown around their heads. A giant marabou stork, looking exactly like the undertaker he was, stood perched in a tree—all agleam in a black coat and a white shirt—ready to dispatch a dead animal at a moments notice. In attendance were several bald-headed vultures, all in the same business as the stork. A helmeted guinea-fowl disappeared into the bush followed by an incredible number of young while some friendly looking black and white wag-tails did their characteristic rhythmic tail-wagging dance from the safety of a tree.

Kandi also thrilled to the music of passionate songsters hidden in the foliage, apparently determined to sing out every hour of day and night. *Trill - trill -trill*, went one Lark: *twee - twee - twee* , answered its mate. *Twitter - twitter*, went the swallows as they staged an incredible aerial ballet—skimming the air at unbelievable speeds, with sudden, but graceful and accurate change of direction.

On the third day of their stay, Kandi sat at the veranda watching the Talek making its lazy way along the sandy bed, khaki-coloured water, trembling in response to the hot afternoon wind.

Across the bank, dead trees, sculpted by lightning, rain and wind stood gauntly against the blue sky. The nearer hills were green, but the distant ones were a misty blue, merging with the azure of the sky. A red, blue and silver-grey gecko lizard appeared at a distant corner and nodded his head at her. Kandi smiled at it, impressed by his gay colours. She moved slightly and the gecko darted off to inspect something else.

She listened to the birds singing and the sound of the wind as it blew through Eden. And at her feet the Talek made its way downstream, unperturbed.

The woman felt surrounded by a vibrant timelessness—the world standing still to listen to itself. Suddenly it occurred to her that Johnny, who had gone to the bookshop, was taking rather long. An uncharacteristic unease came over her in the midst of all this idyllic calm.

SEVENTEEN

FLYING DOCTOR IN THE WILD

JOHNNY HAD GONE to the bookshop to see whether he could get a book to improve his knowledge of predators. Browsing happily through books about animals, he was unaware of the passage of time. The lounge and dining area were almost deserted, with most guests away in their rooms to escape the afternoon heat.

Suddenly a man whose face was a bright red from too much sun and whisky; and two Africans, one very tall and lithe and the other one of medium height but very muscular and powerful looking came into view. The two Africans were gesticulating wildly while the red-faced man was trying to calm them down.

As they moved nearer Johnny caught some of their words:

"Give us our money, we won't go further if you don't give us our money!"

"Listen, you idiots, I am not giving you any money

before we cross into Tanzania. It is too dangerous for us to spend any more time here. The cops are aware that the border is being used as a transit for drugs and you should know just how stiff the penalties are. *Twende!*"

The trio passed the bookshop and spilled out the door into the bright sun outside. Without a second thought Johnny followed them. His curiosity had been roused and he wanted to see and hear more with the vague intention of informing someone in authority.

The three men entered a powerful-looking double-cabin Toyota Hilux pick-up and backed out. The tall one was driving. As luck would have it one of the hotel employees who knew Johnny from one of his many trips to evacuate ailing tourists rode in on a 200cc Honda motorbike.

Johnny ran to him and shouted:

"Emergency! Someone's badly hurt! Let me have your bike. I will bring it back!"

Without allowing the man a moment to collect his wits, Johnny grabbed the handlebars and practically pushed him off.

"*Pole Daktari!* You poor doctors never have a moment of peace now, do you?" he said sympathetically to Johnny's back as it disappeared round a bush.

The Hilux sped towards the Sarova Lodge and Johnny tried to follow it as discreetly as possible. It occurred to him that he was being very foolhardy. A guy could lose his life from this kind of thing. He would stop off at the Sarova and inform them about what had happened. But even as he thought of this, the Hilux veered and drove straight into the bush.

"Bastards! These are the people who are giving our beautiful game-parks a bad name!" Johnny had hoped to reach the rangers' post, which was not far off, to tip them before the guys got too far. He paused momentarily then rode on. As he passed where the pick-up had verred off, someone leapt out of a tree and wrestled him to the ground. They roped him up like a wild animal and threw him onto the back of the Hilux.

"Why are you following us, eh? *Pumbavu!*" With that the short powerful man gave him a mighty kick in the loin. Johnny was sure that the kick had ruptured his kidney. *You only need one kidney to live,* he thought wildly as agony exploded through his body. He rolled onto his side to protect his other kidney, but the man rained blows on his body from every angle as the pick-up lurched on dizzyingly, sending the animals galloping away to safety.

It was the cessation of pain that made Johnny realise that the pick-up had stopped moving. He opened his one functional eye and realised that he was alone. The men were talking outside and he realised that he was the subject.

"I say shoot the bugger!"

"Why waste a bullet on him, *Bwana.* It might even give the cops unnecessary evidence about us! I say dump him in the bush and leave him for the animals to chew." With that they drove towards a particularly dense thicket.

Johnny, meanwhile, tried out his arms and was surprised to discover that the ropes had worked themselves lose, perhaps due to the bumpy movements of the vehicle and the beating he had received. The men came back and Johnny faked deep unconsciousness if not actual death. They grabbed him unceremoniously and threw him into the bush. Johnny allowed himself to fall awkwardly, but red-face gave him a mighty kick to the ribs just to be sure. It took Johnny large amounts of present and future supplies of will-power to keep from screaming at the top of his lungs. The men drove away confident that in the vastness of the Mara, hyenas or other animals would have dispatched the fool long before anyone could find him.

Johnny lay absolutely still until he could no longer hear the growl of the powerful engine, then gingerly he examined his body to find out the extent of the damage. It felt considerable—bumps on the head, no doubt several cracked ribs, fractured jaw, unknown damage to his internal organs. His forearm was badly bruised but otherwise his limbs were intact. He needed them to escape. Death in this jungle was inconceivable. He was newly-married, wasn't he? Surely he owed it to Kandi to stay alive and not die in so stupid and senseless a manner.

A growl followed by a hysterical laugh split the warm afternoon air. The terrifying sound galvanized

Johnny into action. He looked around. The tallest tree was some distance away and he could not take that chance. He had no choice but to go for a less tall but more accessible one. With preternatural strength inspired by thoughts of being ripped apart by a hyena he shinnied up the tree as if he was in the pink of excellent health.

From his vantage point Johnny saw the hyena moving with awkward, but focused determination towards a meal. He felt his heart hammering away in his chest as he tried to catch his breath.

Johnny's hope was that the man whose bike he had taken had reported his absence to the manager or that Kandi would get alarmed and report his absence. He hoped it would be soon. He felt awful and was beginning to get dizzy. *I hope I'm not bleeding internally,* he thought to himself as he wedged himself as firmly as possible into a fork in the tree. *And I hope that it is true that leopards only hunt at night.*

***

BACK AT THE LODGE Kandi looked at her watch again. It was four o'clock. Johnny had been gone for two hours. How forgetful of him, she thought; but she was worried. They had planned to go for the evening game drive as usual and it was unlikely that he had forgotten.

"Maybe he is waiting for me to join him at the bookshop," she said out loud to herself.

She tidied herself, grabbed the binoculars and stepped out into the sun. She walked briskly to the bookshop and went in to look for Johnny. He wasn't there and had not been there for a while. Kandi made her way to the reception to make inquiries. No-one seemed to know what had become of him. Kandi was at the point of becoming hysterical when the man whose bike Johnny had borrowed happened to hear her raised voice.

"But Madam! I am so sorry. Didn't you know that he has been called away on an emergency?" Kandi's heart stopped.

"Emergency! What emergency? We are on holiday —on our honeymoon!"

"I met him while coming in and he grabbed my motor-bike saying that someone was badly injured. I didn't ask him where. He is quite well-known around here, you know, and I thought someone had discovered that he was a guest here and had asked him to help out in an emergency. I'll make inquiries immediately, Madam."

But nobody had heard of any emergency and the telephone operator had received no calls for Dr Courtney. The operator wasted valuable time calling to the surrounding lodges, but no one had heard of an emergency of any kind. It had been a very calm day in the wild.

All that Kandi could think of was that a man on a motor-bike out in the game park was easy prey to practically anything that felt like making an effort. And there was only about an hour of daylight left—it was already some minutes past five o'clock! Her fear communicated itself to the management who immediately organised two search parties and also radioed for extra help from the game rangers.

***

UP IN HIS TREE, Johnny, who was kept awake only by the intensity of his pain and fear, looked at the setting sun. It was a breathtaking sight which he would have enjoyed in a more salubrious state. But all that he could think of now was that soon, the leopards would be at large. And that when it came to climbing trees leopards were in a league of their own.

"Please God, let them find me. I promise never to aspire to anything else but Medicine. In future I shall leave crime-busting to people with stronger ribs and thicker skulls." He clung to the hope that they would find him in good time.

The sun dipped into the horizon, leaving behind a pale golden haze which soon disappeared. And it finally occurred to Johnny with great clarity just what looking for a needle in a haystack meant. It was like searching for one miserable man lost in the Mara. And it was almost hopeless at night.

It got darker, but it was not yet the inky black of the African night, when Johnny saw the lights of a vehicle moving slowly in the night. Johnny yelled at the top of his bruised lungs and watched in disbelief as the lights moved on in the wrong direction. The vehicle had been about a hundred metres away. Real despair stole into his soul for the first time. But even as he tasted its ashy taste in his mouth, the vehicle came round again and this time it passed much nearer. And Johnny, discarding all concern for his damaged ribs and broken jaw to the four winds, screamed like a banshee in the night. The vehicle stopped and then slowly started moving towards him. Johnny kept up the spirited yelling until it was clear that they had accurately localised him. He passed out from sheer relief.

Two lean rangers climbed up the tree and gently disentangled him from his perch. Kandi stood beneath the tree in a state of near collapse.

"Is he alive?" she asked in a trembling voice.

Johnny stirred and groaned and Kandi sighed in relief.

The driver radioed base and asked them to get East African Medical Airlift as fast as possible. Captain Flynn landed his Fokker 10 at the airstrip inside an hour and a half. With him were Ilana Mwandawiro and Dr Ashraf Khan who was the flying doctor on stand-by that day. With even more dedication than usual, if that was possible, they set to work on their colleague. In half an hour they were airborne with Kandi holding Johnny's hand as if it was a lifeline from her to him. Their haste was just as well.

The thin clot on Johnny's bruised spleen gave way and slowly at first, then like a breached dam, he began to haemorrhage. As they approached Wilson Airport, Johnny's vital signs took a nosedive. Ilana opened up the drip to full capacity and began to pump fluid into her now moribund patient. Dr Khan inserted a large bore cannula and began to infuse the first of the two units of blood they had brought with them. It was too small an amount, but at least they had something to begin with. Dr Khan knew an intra-abdominal catastrophe when he saw one.

"Radio on for the hospital to get theatre ready immediately. I don't think he can wait," he said to Captain Flynn who started to give instructions into his head-set with an unusual note of urgency in his customary drawl.

The ambulance moved towards the plane almost before it came to a stop, and loading the patient on, it drove off with its siren wailing. They took Johnny straight to theatre. He was a little more stable for the ambulance had had more blood on standby—and in the twenty-five minutes it had taken them to get to hospital, they had already given him another two units and were on a third.

"Scalpel!" ordered Dr Matagaro, ready scrubbed and gowned—palm open to receive the instrument. *No way am I losing you, my boy. No way!*

Just outside, Kandi was still in shock. Someone had wanted to give her something to sedate her but she had refused, not too politely. What could the man possibly have been up to, she wondered for the umpteenth time? And what under heaven was taking them so long?

She had informed his unbelieving family who had arrived within minutes. Aoro had scrubbed and gone into theatre to assist while Wandia was marching up and down.

It was almost midnight when Dr Matagaro finally emerged.

"Mrs Courtney?" he inquired gently. Kandi lifted her head slowly. She was still not used to her new name. The man was still gowned except for his mask, and in Kandi's overwrought state he looked like an apparition. Her eyes dilated in fear and she could not utter a word. Wandia came nearer feeling that perhaps she had lived for too long already. She was not ready for this.

"No! No! Mrs Courtney. Your husband's going to be just fine. We had to remove his spleen, but who needs a spleen anyway—not my boy, I can assure you…" His voice thickened with emotion and he retreated back into his true habitat—the theatre.

Johnny's recovery was not only uneventful, it was rapid. By the fourth day he could give a statement to the police and by the fifth day he was front page news in the dailies:

FLYING DOCTOR STUMBLES INTO DRUG RUNNERS!, screamed one which also had Johnny's photograph in better days side to side with one of him in hospital with his head swathed in bandages. Johnny's ego did not suffer too much from all this attention, but as Kandi pointed out:

"We pay taxes for such purposes as the employment of a police-force. If I'd wanted to marry a policeman I would have done so, understand?"

"Yes sweetheart," answered Johnny, all sweet docility. But Kandi realised that there would rarely be a boring day around the man she had chosen to marry.

It took almost a year before the police caught up with the man who had kicked Johnny so ferociously. A few months later Interpol caught up with red-face in New York where he had hoped to disappear in the huge seething mix of humanity characteristic of that city. The tall man was still at large.

But Johnny was by then the father of a little person by the name of John III who demanded all his free moments.